John Butler

Electricity in Surgery

John Butler

Electricity in Surgery

ISBN/EAN: 9783337405977

Printed in Europe, USA, Canada, Australia, Japan

Cover: Foto ©Andreas Hilbeck / pixelio.de

More available books at **www.hansebooks.com**

ELECTRICITY.

IN

SURGERY.

BY

JOHN BUTLER, M.D.

BOERICKE & TAFEL:

NEW YORK:
145 GRAND STREET.

PHILADELPHIA:
1011 ARCH STREET.

1882.

PRESS GLOBE PRINTING HOUSE PHILADELPHIA

CONTENTS.

4 CONTENTS.

PREFACE.

THESE few pages are intended as a practical guide for the use of the specialist and general practitioner, and aim at showing the necessity of attaining accuracy of detail in all electro-surgical operations.

The scope of the work precludes the possibility of more than cursory allusion to clinical cases, but is based almost entirely upon the author's own personal experience, and is for the most part composed of articles written from time to time for different periodicals, revised and condensed.

It presumes a knowledge of the rudiments of electro-physics on the part of the reader.

It is confidently hoped that it may be accepted by the profession in the same spirit that it is offered—as the contribution of one man's mite to the cause.

JOHN BUTLER, M.D.,
102 East Twenty-second Street,
New York City.

INTRODUCTION.

Less than twenty years ago, a period within the recollection of the majority of the physicians of to-day, the use of electricity in any form, as a therapeutic agent, was scouted and derided as a quackery; and up to a still more recent period those manifesting any interest in electrology were looked upon with suspicion, and if not actually branded as charlatans, were at least sneered at and avoided by a large majority of physicians.

To-day all this is changed, and electricity is now honorably enrolled among our list of therapeutic agents, and admitted to be one of the most potent weapons we possess, in combating many forms of disease.

As a means of diagnosis, the induction machine and galvanic battery stand side by side with the stethoscope, plessimeter, dynameter, sphygmograph, etc., while the use of electricity in surgery in the treatment of tumors, strictures, and other diseases, in which resort to the knife is inadmissible or undesirable, needs not here be more than alluded to, as it will be fully discussed in the following pages. Within a few years, electro-therapy has made very rapid progress—so rapid, indeed, that works on the subject written but a short time ago are now almost valueless as text-books, containing none of the recent developments.

But although the knowledge of the use of electricity in medicine and surgery has advanced rapidly, it has not kept pace with the progress of electricity in other branches of science. In electro-surgery this is particularly evident. In the books that have been written, although the principles that govern the physiological, chemical, dynamical, and other actions of electricity are admirably given in outline, making these works very useful to the student and practitioner in acquiring a general knowledge of the subject, still the attention of the reader has not in any of them been drawn to the absolute necessity of attaining precision, in operating, precision in the administration of the required dose and no more, precision in carrying out the thousands of little details which tend to make electro-surgery a certain science; so that these works are but of little value to the specialist. The consequence of too much generalization in our literature has been a looseness in operating, inattention to details, neglect of the laws which govern electricity (the knowledge of which gives the only key to success), and has led to much blind and ignorant experimenting, which is to be deplored.

Every electro-plater can calculate to the utmost exactness, just how much silver, gold, or nickel or other metal he deposits on an article in a minute, or in an hour.

Those engaged in the construction of telegraph lines know exactly the amount of current to use on a line of a given distance.

Experts in electric lights will tell you without a

moment's hesitation, the precise expenditure of force necessary to obtain a light of a certain power of illumination.

But practitioners of electro-surgery—how many of them can tell how much current to use on a given case? How many can give even a proximate estimate of the amount of actual current it will take to coagulate the necessary amount of blood to cure an aneurism, will exert sufficient chemical action to produce total destruction of a malignant growth, or will cause enough interference with the nutrition of any tumor to cause its speedy disappearance either by absorption or suppuration, at the option of the operator? Very, very few. And why should this be so? Do not the same natural laws govern the action of electricity in every case? Certainly. The amount of work done is always proportional to the amount of actual current flowing the circuit in a given time, and the amount of actual current always equals the electro-motive force divided by the sum of the resistances. This law of Ohm's is recognized by the electro-plater, by those skilled in telegraphy, and by those engaged in electric lighting. That they must adapt their work to it is evident; for if they do not, and use too little force, the work is not done; if too much, it is overdone, and the expense is unnecessarily increased.

With amateurs in electro-surgery it is different. If in a case of tumor or stricture, too little current be used, and no improvement follow, it is put down as another unsuccessful case, or else nothing is said about it. If too much be used, and the patient die, or be disfigured from destruction of the surrounding healthy tissues—well, it could not be helped, everything was done that could be done under the circumstances, and so electricity earns a bad reputation. If the doctor happens to use just enough current, and a cure results, the fact is heralded as another glorious achievement in electro-surgery, paraded at society meetings, recorded in loose generalizations, and copied from one medical journal to another. This state of things should not exist. We can and should do better; we have most, and by study can obtain all the data necessary to attain precision, and our electrolytic operations *can* be conducted with the utmost exactness.

To illustrate my meaning;—let us suppose a case—say of aneurism. Now, in order to cure this aneurism it is necessary to produce a coagulum that will fill the greater part of its cavity. Nothing less than this will do; that all physicians know; they also know that the galvanic current is one of the most powerful agents we are possessed of for causing coagulation of blood, and to this end the galvanic battery is frequently used. But how is it used? Here is a specimen of an ordinary report of a case: Mr. A. B., æt. 40, admitted into——Hospital on November——, 1876; aneurism of arch of aorta. Four insulated needles connected with the positive pole, and three with the negative of a battery of six cells (or six cells of a certain kind) were inserted into the tumor. After five minutes the current was increased to twelve cells, and allowed to flow for half an hour uninterruptedly. The patient died next day.

What do we learn from this? Simply that the electro-puncture was used on a case of aneurism, and that the patient died—nothing more. We are not given the least information as to the amount of actual current flowing through a circuit in a minute or an hour; consequently we do not know how much of a coagulum was produced by the operation, nor how much was broken up by the with-drawal of the needles.

The amount of current can only be calculated by Ohm's law, viz., $C = \dfrac{E}{R + r}$, so that if $R + r$ are unknown, C. remains still an unknown quantity, even though we know the exact E. Consequently the work done, or, in other words, the amount of coagulum produced, remains an un-known quantity.

For the benefit of those who as yet have not given the subject of electro-surgery much attention, and to make my meaning still more clear, let us follow out a very simple electrolytic operation, viz., the effect of a galvanic current in decomposing water. We are all aware that when a galvanic current is passed through water (the water, of course, being part of the circuit), that it is decomposed, the oxygen being liberated at the point where the metal-lic part of the circuit connected with the positive pole makes contact with the water, and at the point of contact of the negative electrode, the hydrogen is liberated. The rate at which the decomposition takes place, is in the direct ratio of the amount of current flowing through the circuit

in a given time. A veber of current will decompose
.00142 of a grain of water in a second. Suppose, then, we
have a battery of six Daniell's cells, and the internal resistance of each cell is five ohms, and of the external part
of the circuit, viz., the water between the electrodes and
the terminal wires of the battery thirty ohms, how much
current is passing in a second of time? How much water
is decomposed? The equation reads thus:

$$C = \frac{6\,E}{6\,R + r} = \frac{6}{30 + 30} = \frac{6}{60} = \frac{1}{10} - \text{veber}$$

per second. Water decomposed, .000142 of a grain per
second.

Now suppose with the same battery we increase external
resistance to seventy ohms by moving the terminals of the
metallic part of the circuit further apart, what a difference
it makes in the amount of current, and in the amount of
work done.

$$C = \frac{6\,E}{6\,R + r} = \frac{6}{30 + 70} = \frac{6}{100} = \frac{3}{50} \text{ veber per}$$

second. Water decomposed, .0000852 of a grain per second, and so on, every time we add an unknown amount
to the resistance, we diminish the current to an unknown
quantity, and the amount of water decomposed, of albumen coagulated, of tissue destroyed, of metal deposited,
of heat, of light, mechanical motion, magnetism produced,
or of other work done, remains unknown. So the result of an operation on living tissue, performed in the
way above recorded, becomes a matter of chance, the

probabilities of success being decidedly in the minority. How then are we to make it otherwise? By making up our minds beforehand, the effect we want to produce, and by calculating the exact amount of current and time it will take to produce the effect. In order to do this, all that is necessary is to measure the electro-motive force of the battery, and the internal and external resistances of the circuit, knowing beforehand the amount of work that a certain quantity of current will do in a given time. This involves a knowledge of electro-physics, an acquired skill in manipulating the delicate instruments used, the necessity of being provided with the materials for conducting the operation. But success in electrolytic operations can only be assured by complying with the natural laws which govern electricity, and we cannot too strongly urge upon those, who intend making electro-therapy a special study, to familiarize themselves thoroughly with these laws, and acquire dexterity and absolute accuracy in using electrical instruments, before operating on living tissue. By doing so they will do justice to their patients, themselves and to the profession; and acquire that true experience which will prove of value to the profession and to humanity. By not doing so, their operations will only be miserable failures, experience will bring no new knowledge of the subject, they will treat themselves unfairly, those under their charge dishonestly, and bring disgrace upon the cause.

The object of this little work is to supply the deficiencies of our literature, aiming at the attainment of absolute precision in cases treated by electro-puncture, and as far as possible in those treated by external, or surface applications, basing conclusions on the fundamental laws which govern electricity, upon the effects which have been observed produced by certain quantities of current upon the living organism, upon organic material, and upon the chemical decomposition of inorganic matter, and upon clinical experience.

HOW TO PERFORM ELECTRO-SURGICAL OPERATIONS.

Before entering on the details of this subject it may be well to briefly enumerate the various uses of electricity in surgery, as well as the diseases that call for its exhibition.

1. Electricity is used for the sake of its absorbent effects in the treatment of serous effusions, recent effusions of blood or of lymph, cystic tumors with watery contents, subacute and chronic glandular enlargements, and in any case in which absorption is interrupted.

2. On account of its ability to coagulate albumen, it is employed in the treatment of aneurism, nævus, and varicosis; and in cases of morbid growths when the object in view is to produce "starvation" (as it were) of the tumor, by causing small coagula to form at several places within its structure; which coagula act as interrupters to the free circulation of blood through the growth, and interfere with its nutrition so far as to render absorption more easy of accomplishment. Any benign solid growth, the removal or total destruction of which is, perhaps, injudicious, or at least undesirable, may be so treated.

3. With a view of utilizing its escharotic effects, electricity is exhibited in malignant tumors, in hard fibrous strictures of urethra, œsophagus, and rectum, and for the removal by electro-chemical decomposition of any morbid growth, whatever be its structure. From this list we should except osteoid or bony formations, as well as mor-

bid growths which have undergone calcareous degeneration.

4. In virtue of the capacity of electricity to cause muscular contractions—it is often called upon to break up adhesions, as in recent cases of partial anchylosis, etc.

5. For the purpose of stimulating the process of repair, its effects are brought to bear upon indolent ulcers, and flabby granulations, of an ulcerated surface.

Omitting a consideration of the use of the current for the purpose of heating metallic burners, actual-cautery, knives, wire-loops, etc., which will be discussed hereafter, the above may be considered a list of the principal uses of electricity in general surgery.

CHRONIC SYNOVITIS.

Electricity is now very generally acknowledged to be one of the most effectual remedies we possess in dispersing the effusion in this disease; both the galvanic and induced currents have been employed with success. Experienced electro-therapeutists have, however, discarded the latter, and use the galvanic current almost exclusively, on account of its being much more reliable and giving more prompt results.

Now as to the modus agendi; how are we to go to work? Suppose we have a case of this affection involving the knee-joint.

The procedure most generally adopted is, to place a broad sponge or chamois covered electrode on each of the lateral aspects of the affected joint, having previously moistened them thoroughly with salt and water; secure them in position with a few turns of a roller, attach them to the poles of a galvanic battery (any form of cell will do for this purpose), and introduce the current, cell by cell, until the patient feels it sensibly; not so strong, however, as to produce pain; and, if the patient complains of the current being too strong, it should be reduced until the point of an agreeable tolerance is attained. A good rheostat is a convenient accessory, but may be dispensed with, and the only galvanometer we need, is the sensation of the patient. As to the length of time the current should be allowed to flow, it is impossible to lay down a definite rule. There is one thing certain, however, that we cannot do any mischief with a tolerably strong current in such a location, even with a prolonged seance, and we may fall short of our mark by not continuing our application sufficiently long. Therefore, I would prefer in such cases rather protracted seances, say of twenty-five or thirty minutes each. These I am in favor of repeating daily. If, during the continuance of the treatment, the cuticle should be denuded by the repeated application of the electrodes, the location of the contact may be changed by placing one of the sponges anteriorly and the other posteriorly on the joint. During the electric treatment the extension of the limb by weight and pulley, as is usual, needs not be interfered with; nor should we be less assiduous with our internal remedies if actually indicated.

Another method, is, to bandage the joint firmly with a roller moistened with water, in which a little salt has been dissolved, and over this apply a metallic bandage made of thick tinfoil or thin stencil plate. This foil is attached to the negative pole of the battery, and then secured in position by a dry bandage. The positive pole in this instance is a large sponge or chamois-covered electrode, secured either above or below the joint. Otherwise the seance is conducted as in the first instance.

2

This mode of making the application is a very convenient one, and at the same time very effective. It is quite as applicable to the wrists, ankles, and other joints, as it is to the knee, although these latter, as also the fingers, may be as effectively treated by immersing them in warm solution of salt connected with the negative pole.

ENLARGED GLANDS.

The late Dr. Maurice Colles, of Dublin, treated glandular enlargements by use of the feeble currents, generated by small batteries made of zinc and copper wires, wound on wood, covered with cloth or felt, and excited by being moistened with dilute sulphuric acid or vinegar. A piece of metallic foil formed the negative pole, which was placed upon the gland, the positive similarly made on an adjacent part. The application was continued several hours and frequently repeated.

Moritz Meyer preferred the use of the induced current, and, in published cases, clearly shows not only its effectiveness, but also its decided superiority over the galvanic current. Of other authorities the majority are also of this opinion.

As the result of my own experience, I would say, that strumous glandular enlargements yield to the action of the induced current locally applied as they do to no other remedy; still they do not yield rapidly, but from the very first of the treatment *some* improvement is evident. The applications should be made daily, with moistened or chamois-covered electrodes of a sufficient size to cover one of the affected glands. When only one gland is diseased, one pole (it matters not which) is placed on the gland, and the other on an adjacent part. When two or more glands are enlarged, both poles may be employed. The secondary induced current is decidedly to be preferred. As regards the length of each seance much depends upon the location. When the glands involved are situated near the head or neck, it is obvious that neither a protracted seance nor a strong current is advisable, on account of being unduly stimulating to the great nerve centers; but in other locations, strong currents (not painful, however) and long seances should be the rule. Firm and steady pressure ought to be made with the electrodes during the whole sitting. The amount of pressure should not be altered on any account, as the slightest alteration not only varies the amount of current flowing through the part, but an unsteady application makes the treatment very disagreeable to the patient.

A sudden cure is not to be expected. The progress is usually slow and steady; some cases, however, subside tolerably rapidly, until they have diminished about two-thirds, and then come to a stand-still, as it were; the last third diminishing very slowly.

ENLARGMENT OF THE PROSTATE.

Onimus says:* "In pure hypertrophy, electricity has not given us any satisfactory results. But when the sequel of an acute prostatitis, or of a congestive process, the currents bring back the organ to its natural size."

Probably Onimus' want of success may have in a great measure been due to the mode in which he made his applications. He inserted one pole into the rectum and placed the other above the pubes.

In my own practice I have been in the habit of inserting

* Medical Electricity, p. 132.

a metallic-tipped electrode into the urethra, the tip being brought into contact with the prostate, and the circuit established by the other pole (a large olive-shaped rectal electrode) placed above the prostate in the rectum. I have used both currents successfully, and the results of my experience has led me to prefer an alternation of the currents to either one alone. I use both currents at the same sitting, commencing with a galvanic current of about $\frac{3}{1000}$ of a veber, continued for about five minutes, following this with weak induced current (without removing the electrodes) for from five to ten minutes more. In all cases, when the galvanic current is used, the negative pole is the one to place in the urethra, for reasons that will be fully entered into when we come to speak of the treatment of stricture. With the induced current this is not of so much consequence.

HYDROCELE.

We find in text-books a variety of opinions expressed regarding the value of electricity as a remedy in this affection. Some authorities extol it highly, while others say it is worthless except as a palliative, and compare it unfavorably with tapping. The reason of this appears to be, that those who operated successfully, hit upon the secret of success as a matter of chance, and without knowing it; while their more unfortunate confreres did not. What I call secret of success is this: In all cystic tumors with serous contents, where it is necessary to introduce needles into the sac to produce absorption, and at the same time destroy the secreting power of the cyst; the needles should touch the internal walls of the sac, and be moved freely over it, so as to allow the electricity to act thoroughly upon the sac itself. When this is done, and the minor conditions of the operation fulfilled, a cure may be confidently expected. When these details are not attended to, the current will in most instances only act as a palliative.

The mode of operating is this: Insert two insulated platinum needles into the scrotum, observing the rules for inserting a trocar. Allow a current of $\frac{3}{100}$ of a veber to flow, and commence to slowly move the negative needle around, so that the uninsulated part makes contact with as much of the lining membrane of the sac as possible. This being done, repeat the operation with the positive needle, allowing the negative needle to stand still in the fluid.

The strength of the current is a matter of importance; a stronger current might produce serious inflammatory action, and even suppuration, while the weaker one would not attain the object in view at all. A galvanometer should be kept in the circuit, a constant battery used, and as the current becomes greater or less, as it will, according as the needles are approximated or separated, it should be regulated by the rheostat, which should be conveniently situated under the operator's hand.

The whole time consumed in the operation needs not be over ten minutes, even when the sac is large. There is often some inflammatory action succeeding the operation, but I have never seen it progress to such a degree as to be at all alarming; however I make it a practice to keep the patient in bed a few days after the puncture. In one case the patient neglected this precaution, but got along well, without any untoward results. The immediate effect of the operation is a rapid diminution in the size of the tumor; indeed, in every instance, it subsides much more rapidly than when the sac is punctured without the current being used. The

reason of this is obvious: the mixed gases generated by
the decomposition of the water, by their pressure force the
fluid of the cyst through the needle openings into the cellular tissue, where it becomes absorbed, this absorption being
stimulated to a great degree by the dynamic action of the
current. The fact of the fluid being rapidly absorbed
should not form any point in the prognosis, for no matter
how unskillfully the operation is performed, this will take
place, while a cure entirely depends upon the conditions
above described being accurately fulfilled.

OVARIAN CYSTS.

There is no reason that I can see, why the rule just given
for operating upon hydrocele should not apply to other
cysts with fluid contents, e. g., ovarian cysts; due allowance
of course being made for the difference of the size of the
growths in the electro-motive force used. In the case of a
large or medium-sized cyst, it would not be necessary to
apply the needles over the whole of the internal surface at
one sitting. A little can be done at a time.

The operation is performed in this way: Two insulated
long needles, about two inches apart, are made to penetrate
the abdominal walls at the most prominent part of the
growth, one needle to each pole of battery. About $\frac{1}{32}$ of
a veber of current per second, may be used for about ten
minutes at each sitting. The needles are then brought into
contact with the internal wall of the sac, and moved slowly
around as in hydrocele.

In all such operations it is of course most needless to say
that the needles should be very thoroughly insulated. The
reasons of this will be evident when we consider the parts
that are perforated before the needle enters the cyst:

1. The integument.
2. The subcutaneous adipose tissue.
3. Tendinous fascia.
4. Peritoneum.

Now it is evident that while all the current may not be expended on these parts, and recomposition may not entirely take place in them, still they act as a shunt, and action of a great portion of the current is expended upon them, and but a small portion is left to do the work on the internal part of the sac. This in itself ought to be a good reason for insulating the needles, even if we do not take into consideration the danger of producing an eschar in the peritoneum and its coverings.

I said what was almost needless to say that the needles should be insulated. I would probably have left out the "almost," and said nothing about the self-evident facts, were it not that I attended an autopsy, some two or three years ago, of a woman who died of peritonitis from this precaution not having been taken; and that the physician that operated upon the patient actually said at a medical meeting, that, "he thought it mattered little whether the needles were insulated or not."

There is another point I would call attention to; it is this: That the word "electrolysis" has been used to express the effect the current exerts in the cure of this disease. Now electrolysis has nothing to do whatever with the cure, as I think I can make evident to the merest tyro in this subject.

Electrolysis means electro-chemical decomposition, and consequent destruction of a fluid and a semi-fluid. A veber of current is a quantity that will do a certain amount of work; for instance, will decompose .00142 of a grain of water.   The resistance of the circuit in the operation on an ovarian cyst may be made to vary from 30 ohms to 2000, according to the distance the needles are placed apart, and the size of the needles, and the conductivity of the fluid, and may be influenced by a number of other facts which need not be detailed here.   Now suppose we take the average electro-motive force that has been used by the physicians who have operated on these cases; as far as I can ascertain it is represented by 10 Daniell's cells.   Call the electro-motive force therefore 10 volts, and the average resistance (with both needles introduced) 600 ohms, and the internal resistance of each cell 4 ohms.

$$\frac{10E}{40R + 600r} = \tfrac{1}{64} \text{ veber per second.}$$

It will, therefore, take this quantity of current sixty-four seconds to decompose a very small fraction of a grain of water, or coagulate a very small fraction of a grain of albumen; and suppose the operation be continued ten minutes and repeated fifty times, which is more than the average, the amount of current transmitted altogether would only be 468.75 vebers; a quantity which will decompose .66557 of a grain of water; and suppose we even multiply this by 100, what possible influence could the electro-chemical decomposition effected have, in bringing out a disappearance of the tumor?   I would therefore limit the meaning of the word electrolysis to its literal signification, and discard its use in reference to the operation in question, and call this operation "treatment by electro-puncture" to avoid confusion, and the use of one word to convey two distinct meanings.

There is absolutely nothing in the medical literature on this subject that is worth reading.   Dr. Paul Mundé has compiled all the available reading material that bears on it, in the second volume of the Gynæcological Transactions, page 348. It is only a compendium of a blind experiment, from which one can learn nothing, except that most of the authorities quoted were lamentably deficient in a knowledge of the principles of electro-physics.

STRICTURE OF THE URETHRA.

The use of the galvanic current in the treatment of the male urethra was first brought to the notice of the profession by Crussel, in 1847. Mallez and Tripier soon afterwards took it up, and are said to have been quite successful. Many of their cases have been published. Crussel's method of operating was: Having ascertained the size of the stricture and its distance from the meatus, etc., to introduce into the urethra, and down to the stricture, a rubber-covered metallic sound, the metallic tip of which protruded beyond the rubber covering. As soon as the tip of the instrument was brought into contact with the stricture, it was made the terminal of the negative pole of a galvanic battery. The circuit was established by the positive terminal being placed in the patient's hand. The current (?) was allowed to act for ten or twenty minutes every day, until the stricture was cured, which desired result, he claims, took place in from eight to ten days.

Tripier used the following modification of this procedure: On the rubber-covered sound, he used an olive-shaped tip of gold or platinum, and made the circuit by the positive pole, being placed in contact with the pelvis. He employed a current of sufficient strength to produce a decided eschar; and it is said that in many instances he obtained good results.

Dr. Newman,* of this city, slightly modified Tripier's operation, used weak currents, and allowed long intervals to elapse between the applications.

It will be noticed that each of these authorities treated all their cases alike, making no distinction between the treatment requisite to produce absorption of a recent soft stricture, and that necessary to cause electro-chemical decomposition of an old, hard, fibrous one. And although these operators had undoubtedly a large number of successes, they must, judging from their loose generalization, certainly have had, by over-doing or not doing enough, quite a large proportion of cases, which turned out unfavorably. This want of discrimination on the part of the pioneers in this department has led to much blind experimenting by men whose knowledge of electro-physics is confined to the facts that a battery can be purchased for so many dollars, and that the negative pole is good for strictures. These men, after applying their poor battery and illy-adapted electrodes, and finding that the strictures did not melt away under the influence of their magic wand, aided by their acquired skill and technical ability, condemned the use of electricity in no measured terms, and really doubted whether it was of value as a remedial agent in any disease whatever. And not only have they cried down electricity as a remedy, but those whose skill, knowledge, and experience gave them such confidence in it as to use it in suitable cases, they decried, either as idle dreamers, or charlatans and men unworthy of confidence.

This ignorance and egotistical assumption has done much to retard the progress of medicine in other departments (Materia Medica for instance), as we well know, and it has

---

* Archives of Electricity and Neurology, May, 1874.

not been without baneful effects in the department in question, and has undoubtedly done much to prevent electricity for being now the universally acknowledged remedy for stricture of the urethra. But although truth may be bitterly opposed, and may be apparently drowned by prejudice for a time, it is certainly to rise to the surface in the end, and shine all the brighter though having shown its ability to withstand the opprobriums of ignorance and prejudice.

The time is not far distant when electrization, skillfully and scientifically used, will be the universally acknowledged remedy for strictures of the urethra, and in the coming text-books on surgery it will be shown to far surpass the old mechanical means for restoring the permeability of the urethral canal: and the old methods of divulsion, forcible dilatation, etc., will by-and-by be taught in our schools only as a matter of historical interest, belonging to a literature of a bygone age.

The rule governing the treatment of strictures by the galvanic current is in no sense different from the rule governing other electrical operations and experiments, viz.: The amount of work done is strictly proportional to the amount of current used.

Sir Henry Thompson* makes two divisions of stricture, viz.: Permanent and transitory.

He defines a permanent stricture as "a contraction due to organic deposit in or around the walls of the urethra, which has no tendency to disappear by any natural action or function of the body;" and describes a transitory stricture as "a contraction due either to vocal vascular inflammation or congestion, causing temporary narrowing of some part of the urethra; hence inflammatory or congestive

---

* Strictures of the Urethra, p. 64.

stricture is spoken of; or to unwonted muscular action of the voluntary or involuntary fibres, in which case it has been designated spasmodic stricture." He further describes the formation and progress of a permanent stricture (which is the only form we shall discuss in this paper), and says :* "The first effect of inflammation upon the mucous membrane is a swelling or thickening of it, caused by the engorgement of the vessels, then exudation of an albuminous fluid takes place into its substance, and especially into the tissues beneath, which may no doubt become absorbed under favorable circumstances. But when the morbid action persists more or less, plastic material is thrown out, which becomes organized, forming a firm fibrous tissue around the canal, causing adhesion between the mucous membrane and the sub-mucous tissue, infiltrating the meshes of the latter, and even involving the substance of the corpus spongiosum itself; while repeated or long-continued attacks of inflammation may cause it to extend throughout the entire thickness of that body, rendering it tough and dense to an extent, in some cases, almost beyond belief."

From this description it will readily be seen, that stricture is capable of being divided into two stages, the first stage being, when the stricture is recent, soft, and semi-fluid, and the second stage commencing, when the plastic effusion has become organized, and the contraction has grown fibrous, hard and solid. It is necessary that a division of this kind in the progress of a stricture should be adopted, in order to be able to define the entirely different actions required of the current for the cure of recent albuminous strictures, and for those that are hard and fibrous.

Having diagnosed a stricture as being soft and semi-fluid,

---

* Op. cit., p. 69.

by the history of the case, touch, etc., and ascertained the anatomical site of the contraction, the length of the stricture, and the relative size of the contracted portion of the urethra compared with the healthy portions (which latter is best done by Otis's urethra-meter), we are in a position to make an application of galvanism with a view of producing absorption.

The method I adopt is this: Select an electrode insulated except the tip, the uninsulated part being the length of the stricture, and of such a diameter as to make contact with the mucous membrane without exercising forcible distention. It should be slightly tapered toward the end. The insulated portion (also tapering) must be of so great a diameter as not to allow any part of it within the stricture.

The patient being placed on his back, the instrument should be well lubricated, and passed down to, and into the stricture.* When we are satisfied that the active part of the electrode is properly located, we place a sponge connected with the positive pole of the battery underneath the patient's gluteal region, and connect the urethra electrode with the negative. Introduce the current gradually, until the galvanometer shows that $\frac{1}{1000}$ of a veber is flowing. This may be increased in some cases to $\frac{2}{1000}$ or even $\frac{3}{1000}$. Beyond this it is better not to go; it certainly is not necessary to use a stronger current; it only needlessly electrolyses the urethra. As to the length of the seance, ten to twelve minutes will usually be sufficient. The weaker the current the longer the time and *vice versa*. The patient should be

---

* In case there is any difficulty in getting the tip well into the contraction, or when false passages exist, the instrument should be passed through a filiform guide; a channel for which is cut in the tip.

examined in about a week after this operation, when it will
be found that the stricture will admit a larger instrument.
In some cases, several numbers larger. If the contraction
has entirely disappeared, then our object is accomplished;
if not, the operation should be repeated at intervals of
about a week, until the calibre of the canal is restored. In
no case needs pain be produced, unless, indeed, the urethral
canal be very irritable, and then the pain is entirely due to
the touch of the instrument and not to the action of the
current, which relieves the irritability markedly. When a
stricture has become fibrous and hard, such an operation
will not answer.

* The operation I use for fibrous strictures, and for which
I claim entire originality, is a means (which I shall describe
presently) by which a stricture can be divided through its
entire length, at one or more points in its circumference,
through its entire thickness, without pain, without hæmorrhage, without division of the meatus, without tendency to
re-formation, by a means that prevents the divided parts
re-uniting, and so forming a new stricture, and by means
that will so act upon the remains of the stricture as to
hasten the absorption.

It will no doubt be conceded that any operation which
fulfils these conditions, is infinitely superior to any hitherto
used.

---

* This article on the treatment of strictures appeared in full in
the *American Journal of Electrology and Neurology*, October, 1879.
I call attention to this fact, as a physician has written an article in
the *Medical Record* for June 25th, 1881, giving this operation as
his own, and calling it electro-urethrotomy. He also gives a description of my instrument slightly modified, and claims it his own
invention.

The instrument that I have designed for this operation is shown in the engraving. It is a hollow sound, insulated, having a slot about two inches (more or less as the case may require) long; in this slot are a pair of concealed wires which can be made to separate and protrude in their long measurement, so as to form an ellipse by turning the nut from left to right. This ellipse, owing to the great flexibility of the wires, adapts itself to the shape of the stricture. There is a groove and eyelet in the tip, b, to allow the use of the filiform guide. A dial on the staff just above the nut, g, indicates the degree of approximation or separation of the wires in millimeters. A long curved ·instrument is here shown with two active wires; but I have also had others made, short and straight, for operating on the dependent portion of the urethra, and others still, with one active wire.

The mode of using this instrument is: Having ascertained the necessary measurements before described, pass the instrument into the urethra until the centre of the slot corresponds to the centre of the contraction; then turn the nut, g, so as to make the wires separate and firmly press on the walls of the urethra, but without causing distention. Attachment of the battery to the binding-post on the nut, g, causes the wires, e f and c d, to become the terminal of one pole, which should be the negative. The circuit is completed by the positive sponge placed on the nates, as in the former instance. All being in situ, a current of from

$\frac{1}{100}$ to $\frac{1}{80}$, or even more, of a veber is allowed to flow. After flowing a short time, it will be found that the instrument has become loose in the stricture. When this is ob- served the nut, g, should be further turned, so as to make the wires protrude still more, until the instrument becomes tight again. The loosening of the instrument is due to the escharotic action of the current, the water decomposed, and the albumen coagulated, etc. The amount to which the wires can be separated from the centre of the staff after the instrument has been fitted to the stricture represents about half the depth of the eschar produced; that is to say, suppose the wires have each been separated from the staff to a distance of one millimeter, there have been two millimeters in depth of the tissue forming the stricture destroyed, part of which tissue has, during the decomposi- tion consequent upon the action of the current, been given off in gaseous form, part in the form of a viscid frothy material, and part remains as a slough, to go through the usual process of separation after a few days. The size, then, of the piece of tissue destroyed is in depth equal to double the distance the wire can be separated from the centre of the staff, after becoming loosened; and as the electric cur- rent acts equally on all sides of the wire, it is fair to pre- sume, that the amount of tissue destroyed on each side of the wire would be equal to the amount underneath, were the contact equal in both instances; but as the contact is not efficiently kept up laterally, it follows that the de- struction of tissue on the sides of the wire is less than in the direction of the expansion. Say if one of the wires has been separated from the centre of the staff, one milli- meter, there has been destroyed a portion of tissue two millimeters in depth, and two millimeters (in round numbers) in thickness, making no allowance for the thickness of the wire.

I fancy I hear my readers already saying: That is all very well, but how do you know it? How are you going to prove it? I will tell you how I discovered it.

I observed that, when electrolysis was performed on tissue, e. g., fibrous tissue, by needles from each pole of the battery, that the needles from the negative pole became loose, and that if at any time during the operation one of the negative needles were withdrawn, the hole left much exceeded the size of the needle, and, further, that around this hole was a perceptible amount of eschar, which bore a constant proportion to the diameter of the hole. This proportion, roughly estimated, was, that the diameter of the eschar was equal to the diameter of the hole, less the diameter of the needle. Never having pushed the action of the current beyond the production of a slough of a few millimeters for each needle, I am unable to state whether these facts are to be observed in the case of very large eschars; but the proportion holds good in the case of much larger sloughs than it is necessary to produce in any case of stricture. It is evident that if the foregoing data be attended to, and the measurements made correctly, that any fibrous stricture can be wholly cut through electro-chemically at one sitting.

For various obvious reasons this may not be always advisable; or, owing to spasm, a mistake may be made in the measurement of the calibre of the stricture; such being the case, the stricture must again be operated upon, until sufficient electro-chemical action has taken place. The pain attending the operation is but trifling, and in some cases is not complained of at all. The hæmorrhage is never more

3

than often occurs from the passage of a sound, and, in the majority of instances, no bleeding whatever occurs. Of course some trifling inflammatory action follows the operation, but this is nothing to be compared with what takes place when Tripier's method of sloughing out the whole circumference of the stricture is used. Indeed, I have never seen the inflammatory action cause any trouble whatever.· The use of bougies for the purpose of preventing union of the divided surfaces is unnecessary, as the surfaces are not in close opposition, nor is there any tendency to re-formation of the stricture through cicatricial contraction; as it is well known, that a surface healing after separation of an eschar caused by the action of the negative pole, does not contract in healing. The remnants of the stricture, stimulated by the dynamic action of the current, soon become absorbed, and so the calibre of the canal is restored to its normal condition. In the following table the merits of this method of treatment may be compared with dilatation, divulsion, and internal urethrotomy.

SLOW DILATATION BY SOUNDS.	DIVULSION.
A very slow process. Many and frequent sittings necessary.	A good deal of pain. Hæmorrhage..
To be of any effect the meatus must be divided, or else there is no possibility of stretching the diseased part to the normal calibre.	More or less shock.
Tendency to re-formation strong, the probabilities of return being in the majority.	Often urethral fever.
No means of ascertaining whether the urethra is simply stretched or lacerated.	No possibility of telling whether the stricture is entirely torn through, or whether the healthy parts of the canal have been lacerated.
	Division of meatus necessary, also the frequent use of bougies after operation.
	Strong tendency to cicatricial contraction.
	Many sittings requisite.
	No guaranty of cure.

Internal Urethrotomy.	Electrolysis.
Otis's Method.	*Butler's Method.*
Pain.	No pain, or very little.
Hæmorrhage, often profuse.	No hæmorrhage.
More or less shock.	No shock.
Often urethral fever.	But little liability to urethral fever.
The divided parts being clean-cut surfaces in close apposition, frequent tearing apart is necessary to prevent them permanently re-uniting.	The subsequent use of bougies unnecessary.
Division of meatus necessary.	No division of meatus necessary.
Remnants of stricture become slowly absorbed when the divided parts are kept well asunder, but there is some tendency to cicatricial contraction.	No tendency to re-formation by the parts uniting by the first intention.
Several sittings and long after-treatment requisite to cure the stricture.	No tendency to re-formation through cicatricial contraction.
	The stricture can be cured in a few sittings, and but little after-treatment necessary.

· There are a few cautions to be observed in electrolysing a stricture:

1. A galvanometer should be used that will indicate exactly the amount of current flowing.

2. An adjustable rheostat, by which the flow of the current may be steadily kept at the same point, should be included in the circuit, and so arranged as to be quite under the control of the operator.* This is a matter of great importance, as during the process of electrolysis the resistance of the circuit is constantly changing, owing to change in the conductivity of the chemically altered tissues.

3. The electrodes and accessories should be in situ before the current is allowed to flow.

4. The current should be let on gradually at the com-

---

* The rheostat described under the heading "Instruments," is especially adapted for this purpose.

mencement of the operation, reduced gradually at the close
and shut off entirely before removing the electrodes.

When this operation is carefully performed by an ex-
pert, it will readily be seen that it must be a success in all
uncomplicated cases; but when undertaken by an inex-
perienced or careless operator, the field is a good one for
doing an amount of mischief that in other hands would be
avoided.

Other strictures, *e. g.*, those occurring in the rectum,
œsophagus, etc., may be treated on the principles here laid
down. I have treated a large number successfully; most
of which have been reported in detail in various medical
journals. Stricture of the cervix uteri (from the use of
caustics having produced cicatrices, and so interfering with
the permeability of the canal) may be entirely cured by the
action of the negative pole of the battery. Tripier, Poore
and other authorities highly recommend its use, but depend
entirely on the probe-pointed electrode. To those who intend making a study of this subject, I would say, that when
the stricture is recent, the probe-pointed electrode, and absorbent action of the current, will produce the desired result; but (as in strictures of the urethra) when the cicatrices are of long standing, and have become hard, the
cauterizing action of the current will be needed, and a
modification of the instrument described on page 27 will
be a necessity.

The *modus agendi* is similar to that recommended for
strictures of the urethra and needs no special directions.

ANEURISM.

The galvanic current is employed in the treatment of
aneurism for the sake of its effects in causing coagulation

of blood, the object in view being to form a firm coagulation within the sac, which shall fill or nearly fill the greater part of it, and so obliterate its cavity. Now it is evident that as a certain amount of current will coagulate a certain amount of blood in a known time, that the quantity of current and length of time consumed should be, as accurately as possible, proportioned to the size of the aneurism to be operated upon, and that it should be ascertained beforehand, how long it will take a current producing a known deflection of the needle of a given galvanometer (not a galvanoscope) to produce a clot of the required size.* The slower the coagulum is formed, the better will be the result; that is to say, a coagulum formed by the use of a very weak current, transmitted for a long time, is much firmer and denser than one produced in a short time by a strong current. It is moreover not liable to be broken up by the evolution of the mixed gases produced by the decomposition of water of the blood ; nor is there any danger of sending a bubble of these gases through the heart, as the gases being very slowly evolved, rise gently through the coagulated fluid, are carried away gradually in the circulation, and are absorbed by the animal economy, before they can accumulate in quantities sufficient to produce any injurious effect; while the opposite is true of a strong current.

As the clot caused by the positive pole is much firmer in its texture than that produced by the negative, we should utilize this fact in the treatment of aneurism. I have elsewhere† suggested in outline a new method of treating an-

---

* A current of $\frac{1}{100}$ of a veber will coagulate .1397 of a grain of albumen in a minute.

† Text-book of Electro-Therapeutics and Electro-Surgery, second edition, p. 255.

eurism by galvano-puncture, and now propose giving the operation in detail.

Four, five, or six fine soft iron needles, insulated with hard rubber to within a quarter or half an inch of the points, should be inserted into the cavity of the sac, to the part where it is most essential the coagulum should lie; these needles should be about half an inch apart. A single fine needle insulated in the same way should be then inserted well within the sac, at the distance of about an inch, from any one of the first group of needles. The first group should now be connected with the positive pole of the battery intended to be used, and the single needle with the negative. A galvanometer, which will accurately indicate the amount of coagulation per unit of time, should be included in the circuit.

A current that will coagulate not more than about an eighth of a cubic inch of blood to each needle per hour is, perhaps, the best strength suited for practical purposes. The above conditions having been fulfilled, and the circuit closed with the necessary number of cells included, to produce the pre-ascertained amount of deflection of the galvanometer needle, the coagulation commences. After the current flows for a few moments, it will be noticed that the deflection of the needle becomes less, that is, falls from the point required, this is due to the resistance being increased by the oxidation of the needles, by the slight polarization of the negative needle, and by the fact of the coagula in process of formation being a poorer conductor than the liquid blood. When this fall in the deflection takes place, the number of cells should be increased, or else, where a rheostat is used, a number of resistances should be removed, until the galvanometer again shows that the necessary amount of current flows. At this point it should be fixedly kept until the close of the operation. During the procedure the positive needles become acted upon chemically by the acid set free, and converted into chloride of iron, which materially assists in the formation of a firm clot. This fact should be calculated, and the exact value of this secondary electrolytic action carefully estimated before undertaking the operation. As the needles of the positive pole firmly adhere to the formed clot, their withdrawal is liable to break up the clot and so entirely destroy the effect of the operation. This can be entirely avoided by using needles of such a size that it will be necessary to entirely consume the insulated parts of them in the formation of the coagulation; the point at which this total destruction of the points of needles is reached, is readily ascertained by the galvanometer falling to zero, showing that the circuit is broken. The operation is now completed, and the insulated stumps can easily be withdrawn without the escape of a drop of blood. There may be some slight oozing at the point of insertion of the negative needle, and a few bubbles of hydrogen gas may escape; but this is a matter of no moment, and can be arrested by a slight pressure of the fingers for a short time. The pain of inserting the needles should be avoided by the use of a local anæsthetic. After the needles are in position, the patient feels no sensation whatever, as there is no pain produced by the very mild current; and so there is no contra-indication to continuing the operation several hours, during which time the galvanometer should be carefully watched, and the current regulated accordingly.

Poore,* quoting the opinion of Ciniselli says: "The

---

* Electricity in Medicine and Surgery, p. 248.

operation of the galvano-puncture is admissable in certain
cases, it must be employed for internal aneurisms only, and
for such as are too far advanced. Those are the most favorable in which the sac presses upon but has not perforated
the parietes. A large external sac is a decided contra-indication. Sacculated aneurisms having moderately small
openings, indicated by a small bruit, or, better still, by a
double bruit, are the most favorable for operation. The
origin of large trunks from the sac of an aneurism is a
contra-indication."

It is perhaps almost unnecessary to add that where there
is evidence of a general atheromatous condition of the
blood-vessels the prognosis is not a favorable one; but even
where this is the case, the length of a patient's life may be
added to materially by operating at an earlier stage of the
disease.

Where the conditions above stated are all accurately fulfilled, there can be no possible injury done to the patient,
as there is no shock, no pain, no inflammatory action, and
with due care there needs be no possibility of embolism.

· I suggest this operation altogether on theory, and regret
to say I have had as yet no clinical experience in its use.

NÆVUS.

In the treatment of this affection by means of electricity,
the result aimed at is simply coagulation of the blood con-
tained in the network of little vessels which form the hyper-
vascular tissue, with as little action as possible on the surrounding skin and cellular tissue. The result of electro-
puncture properly performed on a superficial nævus is, that
the nævus shrivels, dries up, and forms a scab, which falls
off in a few days, leaving the surface beneath it in a healthy

condition. On deeper nævi the result is somewhat different, as will be shown presently.

For the purpose of describing the details of the modes of operating, and the different results attainable, we may divide nævi into three kinds, viz.:

1. Those which involve the skin only.

2. Those in which the cellular tissue is the seat of the disease.

3. Those in which both skin and cellular tissue are included.

We will consider the last-mentioned kind first. I have treated this form by a great variety of methods, but of late years have given preference to the following: Having transfixed the base of the growth with a number of very fine harelip pins, about an eighth of an inch apart, I make a connection between the poles of the battery and each alternate pin; that is to say, suppose the base of the tumor has been transfixed by eight pins, parallel to each other, I connect the first, third, fifth, and seventh to one pole of the battery, and the remainder to the other. The current may now be allowed to flow, and continued until the growth has acquired a grayish-white, or dull leaden-colored appearance, and has become comparatively quite hard. The operation is now completed, and the pins may be withdrawn. The negative pins almost fall out by themselves, but those attached to the positive (unless made of platinum), having become corroded, firmly adhere to the tissue in which they are imbedded, and require much care in their removal. Reversing the poles for a moment or two just before the close of the operation, will greatly facilitate their removal. Any bleeding from the openings made by the pins, is positive evidence that the coagulation is not complete, and it

certainly is much better when this happens, to re-insert the
pins and continue the seance, than leave the matter for
another operation. No dressing needs be used. After
eight to twelve days the whole nævus falls off as a scab, and
sometimes leaves (especially when the nævus is small) a
fully healed surface beneath; but in the case of a large
nævus there is left a comparatively small, superficial,
healthy ulcer, which speedily heals, and leaves a slight
cicatrix, that is not always permanent and is never contracted when the amount of current used has been strictly
proportionate to the amount of work to be accomplished.
These cases always need the use of an anæsthetic during
the commencement of the operation. I am in the habit of
using nitrous oxide with adults and large children, discon-
tinuing its use during the latter part of the proceeding,
which is quite painless, owing to the tissues having become
numbed by the action of the current. With infants I use
chloroform, as complete and continued anæsthesia is requisite, for obvious reasons.

Naevi which are deeply situated in the areolar tissue,
and do not involve the skin, must be treated somewhat
differently. Insulated needles must be used. The easiest
way of operating is to insert four needles (not too fine) to
near the centre of the growth, the points at which the
needles come in contact with skin being thoroughly protected by the insulation, and the parts of the needles within
the tissue entirely insulated. A mild current and plenty
of time is the best procedure. It is not so easy to tell when
sufficient action has taken place in these as in the preceding
form, so that it is well to take accurately into calculation
the amount of work to be performed, and the amount of current and time necessary to perform it, before commencing

to operate, and to see that this is accurately measured and indicated by the galvanometer during the seance. In very small deep naevi, the result may be absorption of the clot formed, but in the larger ones we generally have suppuration excited by the clot acting as a foreign body, which nature seeks to expel, so the whole of the abnormal tissue is changed into an abscess, which after some days either discharges itself through one or more of the needle openings, or else, in the event of these having become healed, has to be opened with the aspirator. The same rule holds good with regard to the withdrawal of the needles as previously suggested.

In this form no anæsthetic is needed, unless the pain from the insertion of the needles be dreaded, and pain from this cause can be avoided by the use of the ether spray, locally applied. The action of the current, unless too strong, is not felt, as the skin, protected by the insulation of the needles, is not acted upon by the current.

The third form of naevi are those situated in the skin alone, without penetrating the subcutaneous structures, popularly known by the terms " port wine marks," " mother's marks," "birth marks," "blood marks," "strawberry marks," "rose marks," and a variety of other pet names, as they happen to differ in shape, size, color, etc., are readily removed by galvanic current, but require a totally different operation from either of those previously mentioned, and much skill and experience in the technical details of carrying out the operation.

I have had an instrument made, consisting of a number of very fine needles, imbedded in a circular piece of lead, with the points protruding half their length—something like a Baunschiedt's counter-irritant machine. The needles stand about a sixteenth part of an inch apart and are inclosed in a hard-rubber or hard-wood cylinder, which is furnished with an adjustable screw collar, by means of which the depth to which the needles penetrate the tissues can be regulated to a fraction of a hair's breadth. The mode of using it is as follows:

A moistened chamois-covered carbon electrode attached to the positive pole of the battery is brought into contact with the healthy skin adjoining the nævus. The instrument, with the needles adjusted to the depth the skin is to be punctured, is marked, and the required current allowed to flow. The needles need not be forced through the skin, as the action of the current will make them penetrate to the depth required almost by the weight of the instrument alone. As soon as the needles have sunk to their required depth in this way, the action of the current has been sufficient, and they may then be placed on another part of the mark until the whole has been acted upon. A very mild current is all that is required, and as we cannot use a galvanometer, on account of the resistance being varied all the time, and having to make several interruptions to move and replace the instrument—the amount of current necessary cannot be calculated beforehand with any degree of precision; so that the operation requires a degree of nicety in carrying out the minor details. If too great pressure be used on the instrument, the mechanical action will anticipate the electrolytic, and the part is not sufficiently acted in the process of penetration. If too strong a current be used sloughing of the part will be the result, and the same will occur if the action even of a mild current be unduly prolonged.

The object to be attained is the production of small coagula at the point of the needles, which act as barriers to the blood supply, and so cut off the too free circulation. The result of a properly conducted operation is, either a scabbing process of the entire mark, or else a series of small scabs, corresponding to the needle punctures, form and are shed in a few days, leaving the skin in the normal condition.

Marks of a large area, situated on the head, neck, or face, should not be entirely destroyed at one sitting. I never operate on more than two square inches of surface at a time in such cases. It is better to do a little at a time than transmit a current through the nerve-centres for an unduly long time. Complete anæsthesia will be necessary with children and with most adults. However, I have operated on several cases without an anæsthetic. The pain is not severe, but it is of course that the patient should be kept perfectly quiet. It will be noticed that the rules given for performing the above operations, differ from those laid down by most of the recognized authorities, who use the active positive pole exclusively, making the connection by having the negative placed upon an indifferent part. The reason they give for this is, that the positive pole produces a firmer clot than the negative. I do not think the density of the clot is of any consequence in the treatment of nævi, and so in the first two forms I utilize both poles for the reasons that we can affect our purpose with a very much weaker current than with the unipolar method, and the current being transmitted through the nævus only, does not expend its physiological action on the surrounding parts, and in the case of deep nævi, does not leave a con-tracted cicatrix, as occurs when the positive pole alone is used. In skin nævi the operation suggested could not be

performed with the positive pole, for as soon as the needles
touch the skin, they would adhere fast under its action,
and could not be made to penetrate by any reasonable
amount of force; besides the needles would in a moment
become so corroded that the operation could not be completed.

After having tried the operations laid down by authorities, as well as other methods, I have adopted those above
given as being the most practicable, most easily performed,
and giving the best results.

PIGMENTARY NÆVI.

By transfixing the base of a mole with very fine hair-
like needles, about a line apart, connecting them with the
negative pole of the battery, and completing the circuit by
a needle, the terminal of the positive, driven through the
body of the growth, we can obliterate these unsightly
growths without leaving any mark whatever.

In these cases the current acts by coagulating the blood
supply, and so stopping the nutrition, and the result is (as
in capillary nævi) that the growth shrivels, scabs, and falls
off, leaving a level surface underneath, with the skin perfectly smooth and healthy. One or two Daniels' cells will
furnish all the current needed when the growths are small,
and from five to fifteen minutes will complete the operation. No anæsthetic needed, as a general rule.

MALIGNANT GROWTHS.

There has been much diversity of opinion among electro-therapeutists relative to the actual value of electrolysis
in malignant growths; as to how far the destruction of a
cancerous tumor by electrolysis tends to diminish the lia-

bility of a recurrence of a disease. Some authorities assume that while it does not assure positive exemption from a return, it certainly lessens the tendency thereto. Others say it offers no more immunity than does the removal by the knife; and others, again, that it positively irritates the surrounding textures to such a degree that it increases the likelihood of a re-growth. Every man forms his opinion by the results of his experience and while I have no fault to find with those who differ from me, I wish to have the privilege that I am willing to give others; that is, the privilege of stating the opinions I have formed as the result of my experience.

I am firmly convinced that removal of a malignant growth by electrolysis does lessen the liability to a recurrence of the disease; that any case in which operative interference is necessary, electrolysis is the preferable method; that in certain cases where interference by the knife is not to be thought of, electrolysis is advisable. I have had many cases which substantiate these facts; cases which, having been previously operated upon by the knife, recurred in less than three months after the operation; but the secondary, and in some instances tertiary growths having been removed by electrolysis, the patients recovered, and remained free from any tendency toward recurrence. Some of these operations are of several years standing, and speak for themselves as to their value. They represent almost every variety of malignant disease; epithelioma, medullary sarcoma, spindle-celled sarcoma, etc.

That I have failed in preventing recurrence, it is true; but in each case of failure either the whole of the diseased part could not be removed, or else the system was so impregnated with the disease, that the operation was undertaken with a view of prolonging the patient's life, rather than with a hope of the disease not reappearing.

I have no theory to offer as to how electricity acts in preventing a recurrence. It may be that it influences the surrounding parts by stimulating healthy nutrition—the secretion and formation of healthy cells instead of the mistaken cells which form a cancerous growth; or it may be that after electrolysis, the absorbents are placed in such condition that they are unable to take up and replant any of the few cancer-cells that may accidentally remain; or possibly it may be that the wound, after electrolysis, has to heal by granulation instead of by the first intention, and on that account there is not so much probability of the disease being re-grafted at the time of the operation. I am much inclined to hold the first theory, and for that reason, after the electrolytic slough has come away, make repeated applications of the galvanic current (negative pole) to the healing ulcer. This course may be the secret of success; at any rate, it very greatly hastens the process of cicatrization, and prevents contraction of the tissues taking place. In the case of very large growths, or where a large blood-vessel would be included if a slough were caused, or where, from the position, it is impossible to remove the whole of the diseased mass by electrolysis, I sometimes use Richardson's serrated scissors for its removal, and then thoroughly electrolyze the wound, leaving it quite open to heal by granulation; and during this process continue to make applications of the galvanic current as above mentioned. This treatment I have reason to be satisfied with in every respect.

Now as to the mode of procedure: Should we decide to remove the growth by electrolysis, the first object to be attained, is, to so interfere with the blood-supply as to cut off the nutrition of the diseased mass *in toto*, so that it will slough out. Anything short of this will not do—it will only irritate and do mischief. In order to attain this end, the best way is, to transfix the healthy tissue beneath the growth with several fine insulated needles. These must be parallel, and of such a length as to reach through the entire diameter of the part to be removed, and must be placed close together, the closer the better. These should form the terminal of the negative pole of the battery, the positive pole being terminated by one or two thick platinum needles thrust into the body of the growth. The current is now gradually allowed to flow until the maximum intended to be used is introduced, and at this strength it is continued until the effect required is completed. The first noticeable effect is the bubbling of a frothy viscid material through the needle openings, alongside the needles (the mixed gases liberated through the electrolysis of the water of the tissues bubbling through the partially coagulated albumen). After a few moments it will be seen that a whitish-gray eschar has formed around each negative needle. This is most readily observed when the skin is intact. These separate eschars grow larger and larger in diameter as the operation progresses, until finally they coalesce. When this result takes place, we may conclude that the part has been sufficiently acted upon, and that the blood-supply has been entirely cut off. We may now carefully withdraw our needles. The negative ones will be found to have become quite loose, and will almost fall out of themselves. The positive, on the contrary, are more difficult of removal, and firmly adhere to the textures in which they are imbedded. After the removal, the open-

4

ings made by the positive needles are much more inclined
to bleed than those made by the negative. The hæmorrhage,
however, seldom amounts to much, and may usually be controlled by pressure on the bleeding points, applied for a
few moments with the fingers. The chemical decomposition
which occurs during electrolysis most of my readers are
no doubt familiar with, being minutely described in all the
text-books on the subject. We will therefore omit any consideration of this here.

A tumor, after electrolysis, becomes considerably dis-
tended with the gases formed, which have no means of escape. A tumor formed of tissues which are not dense will
sometimes become resonant to percussion.

This distension subsides in a very short time, and the
mass assumes a shriveled appearance. The contiguous
parts become somewhat inflamed, the patient's temperature
rises one or two degrees, sometimes even more, especially
when large growths have been operated upon. The pulse
rises sometimes as high as 120, and within twenty-four to
forty-eight hours falls to about 100. After the third day,
a distinct line of demarcation appears between the eschar
and the healthy tissues, and in from eight to ten days the
slough comes away, leaving a healthy granulating surface
underneath. This ulcer now needs frequent mild applications of the galvanic current, with broad metallic or carbon
electrodes of such a size and shape as will cover the whole
of the denuded surface. This is, so far, the progress of
the average case. Occasionally, however, I have seen the
temperature rise to 105°, and the fever continue high for
several days, in spite of the indicated remedies being
thoroughly exhibited. Occasionally, too, I have seen the
eschar become putrid and require the use of antiseptics.

As a precautionary measure, I am in the habit of snipping away as much of the eschar as possible, about the third day, and dressing the part with a weak solution of zinc chloride, though I have never known the slightest septicæmia to follow electrolysis.

As regards the definite amount of current to be used, there can be no rule laid down, as that depends upon the size, density, and conductivity of the diseased tissue, and bears an inverse proportion to the length of time to be consumed in the operation. I am in favor of a moderate current continued for a sufficiently long time, having reason to believe that such operations give better results than those in which very violent chemical action takes place. All such operations, of course, must be performed under an anæsthetic.

Cases of cancer, which although hopelessly incurable, may be paliated, and the pain much allayed, by the exhibition of electricity in another way.

One or two very fine needles (long harelip pins will answer the purpose very well) should be inserted into opposite sides of the tumor, penetrating well towards the centre of the growth; these may be painlessly inserted by the use of rhigolene or ether spray, as a local anæsthetic, or in many cases even without local anæsthesia being necessary. A very mild current should be allowed to flow through the tumor, the needles being the electrodes. One or two of Daniel's cells, or their equivalent, will furnish amply sufficient electromotive force for any case. After the current flows a few moments, it is by no means unusual to find that the pain has entirely subsided, and that the weary worn-out patient has actually fallen asleep with the needles sticking in the growth.

It is only the first application patients dread. After one has experienced the soothing effects of the galvanic current used in this way, he will beg for its repetition and anxiously look forward to the time for the next application. As regards the duration of each seance, we must be guided wholly by the sensation of the patient. As soon as the pain subsides, the current may be discontinued. This result usually takes place in from five minutes to half an hour, and the beneficial effects last from a few hours to several days. It need hardly be said, that as long as the patient remains free from pain, the application should not be repeated, but each return of pain may be combated by a re-puncture Each successive puncture should be made at a new point, for if made every time at the same point, we soon have an eschar formed, and fistulous openings corresponding to the track of the needles made in the growth, which only add to the suffering, instead of diminishing it.

Once in a while, we will see more than a mere transitory benefit from the treatment; after a few applications the diseased tissue assumes a shrunken appearance, and the patient's health improves in a marked manner. I have not seen much benefit arise from the external application of moistened electrodes, but where the surface is ulcerated much good may be done by using flat metallic electrodes applied to the ulcerated surface, instead of making punctures with needles.

In all cases, the galvanic current is the form to use, as no possible good can come from faradizing the parts, as many are in the habit of doing.

FIBROID TUMORS.

Of course it is quite possible to destroy any benign growth

by the treatment just described, but such a course is not necessary. Fibrous tumors may be treated electrically by one of two methods, at the discretion of the surgeon.

1st. By forming the eschar within the growth of a sufficient size to act as a foreign body. This excites suppuration, the tumor becomes an abscess and the pus is evacuated, etc.

2d. By producing several small coagula within the growth, not sufficiently large, however, to cause suppuration, but large enough to lessen nutrition and lessen the blood supply.*

· Repeated operations of this kind will cause a tumor to become absorbed. There is no doubt that fibrous tumors have been dispersed by simply passing galvanic current through them without puncture. This method is, however, uncertain and unsatisfactory, and under any circumstances needs a long-continued and tedious treatment, and very frequent seances. If, in a given case, we decide to employ the first-mentioned method, we introduce several needles insulated to within about half an inch of their points (according to the size of the growth), into the body of the tumor, as near to the centre of the growth as possible. The needles should be close together, but great care should be taken that they do not touch each other. One or two of these needles should be connected with the positive pole, and the remainder with the negative. Enough of current should be allowed to flow to produce an eschar of the size we desire in a given time. This must be carefully calculated, for if we use too much current or protract the se-

---

* At the December meeting of the Medico-Chirurgical Society of New York, I reported thirteen successive cases of uterine fibroids successfully treated in this manner.

ance, we slough out the whole growth and perhaps some of the adjacent tissues. If too little, the object is not attained. An anæsthetic is not always necessary, but the part should be sprayed while the needles are being introduced, in case where an anæsthetic is not used.

In instances where the second method is the chosen one, as it generally is, we should proceed as follows.: Insert several insulated needles within the growth, as far apart as possible, but as nearly equidistant as practicable. The insulations should penetrate well within the skin or mucous membrane, but it is of course essential (considering the objects in view) that the needles should have long uninsulated points. One of the needles may now be made the positive terminal, and the other the negative; or each alternate needle may be attached to one pole, and the remainder to the other, at the option of the operator. The needles attached to the positive pole should be made of platinum, otherwise there is much difficulty in removing them; besides secondary electrolytic action takes place, which tends to suppurative action around the tracks of the needles, which of course should be avoided. We only require a mild current regulated in strength according to the work to be done; that is, to the size and number of the coagula we wish to produce, and as that altogether depends upon the size of the tumor, it is obvious that no explicit direction on this point can be given, as it is impossible to average such matters.

This operation has to be repeated again and again at intervals, until the desired result is attained. There is never much inflammatory action after a properly performed operation, but always some; and I make a practice always of waiting at least a week after the inflammatory symptoms of one operation have subsided before making a second. This method is applicable to fibrous growths in any part of the body. I have successfully treated many uterine fibroids, both submucous and subperitoneal, by its use, as well as fibroid goitres and tumors elsewhere attached.

FATTY TUMORS.

Although it is quite possible to destroy these tumors by electrolysis, it is not by any means to be recommended as the best mode of treatment; for fatty tissue, conducting electricity only through the medium of the small amount of water it contains, is a very poor conductor, and can therefore scarcely be called an electrolyte. It follows from these facts that the tension of current requisite to produce even a very small eschar must be very great, and the length of time consumed in an operation proportionally great. These facts in themselves would not be serious objections did removal of such growths by electrolysis possess any manifest advantages over excision; but as enucleation by the knife is a very simple operation, by which the whole of the adventitious mass can be at once removed, and the tissues covering the growth immediately brought together, which unite generally by the first intention, so I venture to doubt that any instance ever occurs where it is at all desirable to remove these growths by electrolysis.

ADENOID TUMORS.

Electrical treatment of these tumors may be undertaken with one or three objects in view:

1. To promote absorption and stimulate the normal nutrition of the part.

2. To produce small eschars within the growth, which

shall act as barriers to the free blood-supply and so cause a diminution in size, and finally absorption.

Or, 3. To cause it to terminate in an abscess in the manner previously described under the heading, "Fibroid Tumors."

The details of the treatment require to be essentially modified according to the end we wish to accomplish.

When we desire merely to stimulate absorption we simply apply a moistened electrode (negative) to the tumor, the electrode being of such a shape and size as to cover the entire growth, and the other electrode upon the skin adjoining. This latter should be constantly moved in a direction around the growth during the seance, and not allowed to remain long on one part. Daily s ances give the best results.

The secondary induced current has made several cures, and is preferred to the galvanic by many authorities.

If this treatment succeeded in all cases, it would of course be the most preferable mode of operating; but very often it will not. It then is a question to be decided by the surgeon, when in a given case it is best to make several eschars within the tumor, and repeat the operation several times, until the end is occomplished, or make one large eschar which will cause the growth to suppurate. The mode of operating with either object in view, is essentially the same as that described in speaking of the treatment of fibroid tumors; but adenoid tumors yield the action of the current much more readily than do fibroids, therefore we do not need so much current in an operation on the former; and we should take great care when operating with the results of the second mode of procedure as our aim, lest we cause the whole growth to slough out, by using too strong a current, or unduly continuing its action.

CYSTIC TUMORS.

In the preceding pages I alluded to the treatment of cysts with serous contents and their successful treatment by electro-puncture. We will now, therefore, only consider those with pultaceous or semi-solid contents. These are difficult growths to electrolyze. I mean to so electrolyze as to destroy the sac and contents without at the same time destroying the skin covering the tumor. Electrolysis of the contents of the sac will not do. If the sac is not also destroyed, it will refill, and so cause a reappearance of the tumor, and if the sac is a thick one, as it so often is, by using a more powerful current than is requisite we cause an eschar of the surrounding and superjacent tissues. I do not know of any rule by which to hit the happy medium, except that taught by long experience. Nor do I know that electro-puncture has any advantage over excision, except that it is not so dreaded by a nervous patient.

ULCERS.

So far we have only discussed the destructive action of the current. We now have to consider it from another point of view. It is well known that electricity has the power of evoking function, of stimulating functional activity, of promoting healthy nutrition. With these objects in view, it is often made use of in the practice of medicine. In surgery, in the treatment of indolent ulcers, these effects are apparent. Under the influence of the galvanic current, old-standing indolent ulcers that have resisted almost all kinds of treatment, seem immediately to take on healthy action, granulations spring up, and cicatrization advances in a manner little short of magical. Now as to the mode of using the current. There are numerous methods de-

scribed in the various text-books, all of which are of more
or less value. There is one, however, that has not been
described, and one which I prefer to all others; it is carried
out as follows: I apply a piece of rather thick tin-foil to
the ulcer, which it should accurately fit. Another piece of
foil covered with moistened lint is applied to adjacent surface; the first piece of foil is now made the negative pole
of a small chloride of silver cell, and the other piece of foil
the positive terminal. The part should be bandaged so as
to retain the pieces of foil in their places, and then the current allowed to flow. The application may be continued
for hours or days, as the indications require. A plumbago
rheostat included in the circuit answers admirably to regulate the flow of the current. The sensation of the patient
is here the safety-valve and galvanometer. The current
should not be perceptible to sensation, but should be kept
just below the point at which burning is felt. If there be
the slightest burning sensation there is too much current
flowing and destruction of tissue going on. The rheostat
regulates this to a nicety, and after a little instruction the
treatment, to a great extent, may be safely left in the
hands of an intelligent nurse, or of the patient himself.

THE PERMANENT REMOVAL OF SUPERFLUOUS HAIR BY ELECTROLYSIS.

To those who have not given this subject much attention,
the removal of hairs may at first sight appear to be a
very trivial matter. A moment's reflection, however, will
dissipate any such view of the case. When we consider
the continual indescribable torture that patients afflicted
with trichiasis suffer, which in many cases is at the
most only capable of being temporarily palliated by

the removal of the offending eyelashes, any operative measure that promises to give a reasonable hope of a permanent cure, is certainly deserving of our most careful consideration. Women too, to whom nature has been unwelcomely generous in bestowing upon them the anomolous hirsute appendage, known as a beard, are subjects for our pity and commiseration; for although there are some of the sex ready on all occasions to don the garments of our gender, there are but few who are not willing to undergo any treatment to effectually rid themselves of the masculine ornament they are compelled to wear.

Dr. Geo. Henry Fox, of this city, in the Medical Record for March 22d, 1879, gives a description of an electrolytic operation which he found to be successful in the removal of these growths.

His operation may be described as follows:

Each hair is operated upon separately. The hair is seized by means of a pair of forceps and extracted; a very fine platinum wire, or a fine needle the terminal of the negative pole of a galvanic battery, is then introduced into the hair follicle; and when the circuit is completed, the current is allowed to flow until the hair papilla is destroyed, which result, he says, is known to have taken place, by the escape of a viscid whitish froth (the result of electro-chemical decomposition of the papilla) around the needle. When the hair is coarse, the doctor insists upon the extraction of the hair previous to using the battery, but says, that "in the case of fine hairs this is unadvisable," as "often when a fine hair is extracted, it is not an easy matter to set the mouth of the follicle." The author of the paper alluded to, credits Dr. Mitchell of St. Louis with being the first to suggest the use of electricity for the purpose (in trichiasis), and also quotes Dr. H. G. Piffard as having reported two cases of hairy naevus successfully treated, and remarks that this is about the sum total of the literature of the subject.

The objections to the operation described are these:

1. We have no means of ascertaining whether the hair papilla is totally destroyed or only partially so, and if only partially, the result aimed at is not attained. The escape of viscid froth is no evidence that the hair papilla has been sufficiently acted upon.

2. The great difficulty of seeing the follicles, hair, and results of the chemical action thereon. The doctor says: "The use of the lens has been recommended, but as both hands are generally employed, I cannot see how it could be conveniently used, unless fitted to the eye."

3. The removal of the hair by mechanical means, previous to the operation, deprives us of a valuable means of ascertaining whether the amount of electrolysis has been sufficient to destroy the follicle or not.

Being dissatisfied with the operation and its results, I made a number of experiments with different shaped needles, and different forms of magnifying glasses, and modes of procedure; and have adopted the following method of operating, not only on account of its giving the best results, but also on account of its comparative ease with which even a tedious sitting can be borne by the patient, and the greater facility it gives the operator.

The patient being seated in a chair in a semi-reclining position, the head well supported, the face opposite a strong light. The operator selects a hair for the first attack, takes hold of it with a pair of forceps, making it tense by gentle traction.

A moistened sponge electrode from the positive pole of the battery having previously been placed on the back of the neck, or fixed at some other convenient adjacent spot; a three cornered needle with sharp cutting edges set in a suitable handle and attached to the negative pole of the battery, is made to enter the hair follicle, alongside the hair, care being taken to make the needle penetrate to the entire depth of the follicle. The action of the current soon causes a few bubbles of the viscid froth alluded to, to be observed. As soon as this evidence of electrolytic decomposition manifests itself, the needle should be rotated a few times, so as to cause the sharp corners of the needle to scrape away the debris, and allow electrical contact with a fresh surface. The operation is continued until the hair becomes quite loose, and comes away with the slightest traction, the whole operation lasting a very much shorter time than it takes to describe it. The operator proceeds with the next hair in like manner, and so on with the whole series as many as there are to be removed, or as long as the patient can bear it. It is by no means a painful procedure (except in trichiasis), but is usually complained of as a disagreeable sensation.

There is a great difference in patients, however, in this regard; some will tolerate a seance of half an hour or even more, indeed, I had one patient who stood it, or rather sat it out, unflinchingly and uncomplainingly for over an hour, and would have allowed the seance to be continued much longer, but that the operator's eyes became so tired that it was impossible to proceed. I should not omit to mention that I use a modification of a jeweler's magnifying glass which I had made for me by Meyrowitz Brothers, the well-known opticians. It consists of a lens with a four inch focus set in a cork cap, for the sake of lightness, and made of such a shape as to fit the eye, and is readily held there as a single eye-glass is made to do.

Even with the lens, the operation fatigues the eye; but without it, it is almost impossible to continue the seance uninterruptedly for over ten or twelve minutes, and then it must necessarily be done in an unsatisfactory manner, as it is impossible to see how the details are being carried on.

With the lens, a skillful operator ought to be able to destroy about three or four hairs to the minute, and continue the seance half an hour. It will be noticed that I have laid great stress upon the non-removal of the hair previous to the destruction of the papilla; this is one of the principal points in the operation, for as long as the hair remains in, we have a positive guide as to the direction of the follicle, and when it becomes loosened, from the action of the current, it may be taken as almost proof that the papilla has been entirely electrolyzed. I use the word "almost" advisedly, as about ten to twenty per cent. of the hairs acted upon return, and have to be electrolyzed the second time.

The points of the operation for which I claim originality are: the shape of the needle, the rotatory movement thereof, the construction of the lens, and the mode of holding it as adapted to its special use; the advisability of leaving the hair in situ, until the chemical action of the current effects its loosening. The advantages of all of which I hope I have already made apparent.

ASCITES.

In the *Maryland Medical Journal* for December, 1879, there appears a short article from the pen of M. J. Glax, on the treatment of ascites by faradization of the abdominal muscles. He says: "In the five observations made under this simple treatment, the quantity of urine increased on the second, third and fourth days from 200 to 3,000 grams, from 70 to 800 grams, from 2,000 to 24,000 grams respectively. The method consisted in making all the muscles of the abdomen contract under the influence of feeble faradic currents. The seances lasted from forty to fifty minutes." This is evidently a vastly superior operation (or rather series of operations) to tapping and would be naturally much less dreaded by the patient. Why not give it a trial? It seems to me that the electro-massage machine is just the instrument for such a condition, giving in addition to the electricity, the effects of kneading, manipulation and the transmission of mechanical vibrations, certainly valuable auxillaries in the treatment of such cases.

In such conditions the strength of the current only requires to be administered with proximate exactness, the sensation of the patient guiding us as to the strength of the current to be used; it being unnecessary to increase it beyond the point of an agreeable tolerance, and the machine being so readily and easily manipulated, the carrying out of the details of the treatment may be left in the hands of an assistant.

HIP DISEASE.

To relieve the muscular spasm and pain incident to this disease, electricity will be found a valuable ally, and when combined with rolling and kneading the affected muscles, its effects will be more quickly evident. I am in the habit of prescribing the use of my electro-massage instrument.

While the contracted muscles are being rolled and kneaded with the instrument, firm contact of the flat chamois-covered electrode to an adjacent part, is to be secured. The treatment at the commencement of a seance should be very gentle, and afterwards, as a tolerance is manifested, more force can be employed; *but pain should not be produced.* Only very short seances are necessary, but they should be frequently repeated until the desired result is obtained. By this treatment, not only is the pain allayed and the muscular spasm relaxed, but the nutrition of the limb is increased; and I have no doubt but that through these effects taking place, the disease itself is ameliorated.

SPRAINS.

Dr. George K. Smith, of Brooklyn, I believe, was the first to make experiments in this direction. He found that applications of the induced current to the injured part relieved the pain and reduced the swelling. This led others to adopt this mode of treatment, and now the faradic current is generally recognized to be the most potent remedy we possess in the treatment of these accidents.

It may be used in a variety of ways. Probably the best mode is: To bandage the joint with a wet roller bandage, cover this with a layer of tin-foil, which is kept in place with another bandage (a dry one). To the tin-foil is attached one of the poles of an induction machine (it matters not which), the other pole with a large electrode attached, being placed on an adjacent part. The current is allowed to flow very gradually, commencing with a minimum and *gradually* increasing until it is pleasantly perceptible. The slightest increase beyond this point gives great pain, owing to the current producing muscular contractions which cause movement of the injured part. This of course must be avoided.

In cases where the ankle or wrist is the affected joint, the tin-foil and bandage may be dispensed with; and for the local electrode, a vessel of warm water to which a little salt has been added may be substituted. The joint being immersed in the water which is made the terminal of one of the poles, the operation otherwise proceeds as above directed.

My electro-massage instrument can be used as the source of the current with good effect.

BURNS.

The pain of superficial burns may be greatly mitigated by either form of current, the galvanic being the preferable form, as its effects are here much more prompt than the faradic.

The method of application is to immerse the burned part or limb in a liquid, any conducting liquid may be used; I prefer a warm solution of carbonate of soda (which has been so highly recommended as an application to burned surfaces). This solution is made the terminal of the negative pole of the battery—the position being brought into contact with a neighboring part.

In case the part injured is in a position that it cannot be readily immersed, the wet bandage, covered with tin-foil (as directed for the treatment of sprains) may be used. A mild current of about five millevebers may be allowed to flow until the pain is abated, when it should at once be discontinued. One application will usually be found sufficient.

5

CICATRICES.

The constant current has been employed to absorb the cicatrices left by burns, caustics, etc., as well as for those produced by extensive mechanical laceration of the surface. More or less success has followed its use. The current is here used for the sake of its absorbent effects. The mode of procedure is very simple, and requires but little skill to carry it out properly. A moistened sponge or chamois-covered rheophore, of such a size as to cover the entire cicatrix, is applied and fastened to the part. This is connected with the *negative* pole of the battery, the positive rheophore making contact with a neighboring part, and so arranged as to be conveniently moved from time to time during the seance. The current is now gradually turned on, until the patient feels it perceptibly, but is not of such a strength as to produce pain, merely a sensation of warmth, which is more agreeable than otherwise. The positive electrode is moved every two or three minutes to a fresh surface, and about fifteen to twenty minutes consumed in the sitting. Daily applications give the best results.

ELEPHANTIASIS.

Beard and Rockwell and other authorites have suggested the employment of the galvanic current for the treatment of this disease. As yet, however, there has not been sufficient experience in its use to decide as to its merits. The following notice appeared in the *Therapeutic Gazette* for June, 1881:

"Dr. Rino, of France, has reported to the Medical Academy of Paris, that two Brazilian physicians have treated cases of this disease by the galvanic battery, composed of from six to sixty cells, increasing its power grad-

ually. The sensitiveness of the part into which they introduce needles, before the electric current came in contact,
was secured by means of local applications of chloroform.
They report great success, and are encouraged to further
use of this means in this affection."

Having had no clinical experience in the treatment of
this disease, of course I can give no directions as to how to
proceed to use the current. I am quite in the dark as to
what effect these Brazilian gentlemen intended to produce
by the introduction of the needles into the tissues. If the
result aimed at was the stimulation of healthy nutrition,
one would think that the external application of large, flat
electrodes would be far preferable to the introduction of
needles.

PAIN IN GENERAL.

Even when the current has no relation whatever to the
pathological condition, pain may be often ameliorated by a
judicious application of either the galvanic or induced current. The former has greater pain-allaying influence than
the latter. As regards the dose, no definite rule can be
laid down. Mild currents are most generally useful; probably three millevebers would be about the average necessary, but occasionally we meet with cases where a powerful
current is essential to produce the desired effect. Touching
the duration of the seance, an excellent rule to follow is,
not to continue the seance after the pain is relieved, nor
repeat the dose while the patient is free from pain.

SPONDYLITIS (POTT'S DISEASE).

Some authorities dwell on the good results obtained by
galvanization of the affected vertebræ in this disease. From

my own limited experience I cannot offer any definite opin-
'ion as to its efficacy as a remedy.   Still it is not unreason-
able to suppose, from what we know of the effects of galvanism in promoting healthy nutrition, that it would act
beneficially in arresting the progress of this disease. Beard
and Rockwell advise that the positive pole be applied over
the seat of the disease and the negative at some point
above or below, but say nothing about the strength of the
current to be employed or the frequency of the treatment.

LATERAL SPINAL CURVATURE.

Having had a large experience in the treatment of this
affection by electricity, I can speak more decidedly. Faradism, and recently electro-massage, has done much in my
hands to relieve the general debility with which the affection is usually associated; and to give tone to the weakened
relaxed muscles on which the disease depends. I am in
the habit of using frequent applications of a current strong
enough to make the muscles visibly contract, at the same
time avoiding painful effects.   I think the general application of electro-massage gives better results than faradism as
usually applied.   Some cases are most benefited by daily
applications of from twenty minutes to half an hour; others are fatigued by having the treatment repeated thus
often.   In all cases a good rule to follow is: When after
the first treatment there follows a sensation of languor or
fatigue, not to repeat the seances at too close intervals,
but to allow a sufficient period of repose between them.

TALIPES.

Faradization of the paretic muscles is very useful in the
treatment of this deformity.   The electro-massage instru-

ment has at least the advantage over the ordinary faradic machine, that it can be applied by the mother, or attendant of the patient, under the physician's directions. My mode of applying it is: to place the flat electrode under the nates and roll and knead the affected muscles with the drum of the instrument, until the skin assumes a decidedly pink color; this to be the signal that the seance has been sufficiently long. The treatment to be repeated once or twice daily. There is not the trouble in making electrical applications to young children that might be supposed. After the first application, most of them seem to enjoy the sensation; and it is only when they have a repugnance to the operator, or when the latter is so awkward in administering the treatment as to cause them pain, that they raise any objection or interfere with the progress of the procedure.

There are no doubt a number of other surgical difficulties in which the transmission of electricity would be of service, but I think I have here embodied those in which with the light of the experience we now have, it has been of positive and demonstrable service. A discussion of the treatment of varicocele, hæmorrhoids and varicose veins by electrolysis has been purposely omitted, as galvano-cautery gives far better and more prompt results. This latter will be considered in its proper place.

OPACITY OF THE VITREOUS BODY.

It was not intended when commencing this work to make any allusion to diseases of the eye, owing to my rather limited experience in their treatment. I feel, however, impelled before closing this section, to call attention to the remarkable successes of M. Teulon in clearing up opacities of the

vitreous body by means of the galvanic current. In the
Medical Press and Circular for November 9, 1881, he
gives the results of twenty-four cases treated, twenty-two of
which were cured. He applied the positive pole over the
closed eyelids, and the negative to the mastoid process, or
over the superior cervical ganglion of the sympatheticus.
The duration of each seance was two minutes, and only
weak currents were used. He says that every degree of
opacity can be removed by this treatment, unless it should
have assumed a confirmed form of hypertrophy.

GALVANO-CAUTERY.

Electricity being a mode of motion, is capable of being converted into other modes of motion, viz.: heat, light, chemical action, magnetism, mechanical motion, etc. In the operation known as galvano-cautery, the electricity is converted into heat, and it is the heat we make use of in our cautery operations and procedures, and not the electricity, which is only used for the purpose of generating the heat. The force of the current being expended in heating the wire loop, cautery knife, dome, or other instrument, is not transmitted through the tissues with which these instruments are brought in contact, as many who ought to know better suppose, but is simply employed as the most convenient means of bringing these instruments to the proper temperature to secure their cauterizing effects and of retaining them at that temperature during an operation.

When a current is caused to travel through a conductor, the conductor becomes heated, the heat produced being proportional to the resistance of the conductor and the square of the current transmitted. From this it will be readily seen that when the resistance of the circuit is very low and the square of the current very small, the increase of temperature may be so slight as to be imperceptible; but when, on the contrary, a part of the circuit has a high resistance, and the square of the current traversing is also high, the temperature of the part of the circuit having the greatest resistance becomes greatly heated. When the re-

sisting part of the circuit is metallic, it may be made incandescent or even heated to melting point. It is essential
for cautery purposes to select a metal that when heated in
contact with the air, does not readily become oxidized,
which can be heated to whiteness before it reaches the
melting point, of high specific resistance, and perfectly
ductile and malleable. The only metal having all these
qualities is platinum, and it is for these reasons that platinum is employed for the active part of cautery instruments.
Those who are not familiar with the construction of these
instruments, will find them described fully under the head
of instruments.

There is no operation which it is possible to perform
with the knife, which is not also possible by means of
galvano-cautery; on the other hand there are some few
operations which are not possible with the knife, that are
not only possible, but practicable with the cautery, as I
hope to show hereafter. I do not wish to be understood to
say, that the galvano-cautery forms a desirable substitute
for the knife in the majority of cases, for the reverse of
this is true—galvano-cautery has only a small field of usefulness in surgery, and is only to be used where a bloodless
amputation is essential, or where searing of the tissues is
necessary.

The galvano-cautery has been used by Dr. Paul Burns,
of England, in eight amputations of the thigh, two of the
leg, one of the forearm and one of the finger. Bourdon
Amussat and Verneuil have used it repeatedly in trache-
otomy. I have removed the breast in three cases by its use.

In such cases a bloodless operation is not essential, nor
is searing of the parts necessary; furthermore the heated
platinum wire loop in cutting through fatty tissue becomes

so brittle that it readily breaks, the fat melting by the
heat, runs over the skin of the patient, producing painful
burns when it comes in contact, a matter that cannot be
wholly prevented even by the utmost care; the resulting
wound cannot possibly be made to heal by the first intention. For these reasons I certainly prefer the knife in
such operations, and have entirely abandoned the use of
the cautery in their performance. But in amputations of
the tongue, cervix uteri and penis; in the removal of
pedunculated tumors and hæmorrhoids, for the cauterization of fistulæ, sinuses, lupus; for the internal cauterization
of tumors and for controlling hæmorrhage from vessels
that cannot readily be ligated, galvano-cautery has a field
of usefulness in which it is unexcelled by other means.

AMPUTATION OF THE TONGUE.

The removal of any part of the tongue by the knife is
an operation dreaded by the surgeon, on account of the
hæmorrhage that ensues, for if bleeding should not occur
in sufficient quantity to endanger life, it is always of necessity copious enough to fill the mouth and preclude the
possibility of the further steps of the operation being performed with any degree of precision, and the patient having
to frequently rinse the mouth, his volition is essential, so
that an anæsthetic cannot be employed. Removal of the
organ with the chain ecraseur, while a less bloody operation, is open to the same objections in a less degree with
the further objection of dragging into the instrument some
of the healthy part of the organ not intended to be removed, and of leaving behind a contused and lacerated
wound.

The galvano-cautery has none of these objectionable

features. The diseaséd part can be cleanly severed without the loss of one drop of blood, without laceration of tissue, and admits of the patient being fully anæsthetized; advantages that must be appreciated by every surgeon. When a transverse portion of the tip of the tongue has to be removed, the operation is very simple. The platinum loop having been passed around the organ, it is drawn snugly but not too tightly at the point where the separation is to take place; the tongue is then to be drawn slightly forward by a double tenaculum in the hands of an assistant, and the battery attached, making the loop a part of the circuit, which latter on becoming sufficiently heated, is made to cut slowly through the organ by means of the mechanism in the handle of the loop holder. The traction on the loop should be slow, so that the mechanical action may not anticipate the cauterizing effect, and the parts become torn and lacerated in consequence. The wire should not be too hot, or it cuts through too quickly, and the stump, through not being sufficiently seared, is liable to bleed profusely; nor should it be insufficiently heated, for then the stump and surrounding parts become inflamed through being burned by radiation through continued contact. In all cases the surrounding parts should be protected from accidental contact with the heated wire. I have had small strips of box-wood made of such a shape as not only to afford thorough protection to the surrounding parts, but also to act together as a mechanism to keep the mouth open during the operation.

No rule can be laid down as to the degree of heat to which the wire should be brought for operating; it is a matter to be learned only by experience. The battery power that will bring a wire to a white heat in contact with the air, will not bring it to any such temperature in contact with the tissues. The speed at which it cuts is the best test, and the most advisable speed to use has to be learned by practice. In any case it is well to test the battery by drawing the heated loop through a piece of raw meat previous to any operation.

After the part is removed there will be a slight eschar left, which comes away in a few days, leaving a healthy granulating ulcer which rapidly heals without very much attention. A carbolized lotion may be used to correct the fetor of breath which always exists after these operations.

When a lateral part of the tongue has to be removed the organ may be transfixed with a needle, threaded with the platinum wire which is to form the loop. After the wire is drawn through, the needle being liberated, the ends of the wire are inserted into the tubes of the cautery handle. Contact with the battery then is to be established, and the tongue split to the tip. The lateral part to be amputated, is then encircled with the wire, and removed in the manner directed for amputation of a transverse part.

The most convenient size of wire to use is a No. 20 or 21 Stubbs Guage. Too thin a wire will not retain sufficient heat and is liable to be broken; while too thick a one is not only difficult of manipulation, but requires a great amount of current to heat it, and increases the liability of burning by radiation. The directions for manipulating the battery will be found in another part of the work under the heading "Instruments."

AMPUTATION OF THE CERVIX UTERI.

This operation may seem a very simple one to those who never performed it, but having removed this part of the uterus a great number of times, I am in a position to say, that it is one of the most difficult in electro-surgery to do as it ought to be done. It is very well to say that all you have to do is to encircle the cervix with a loop, and the battery does the rest. This is by no means the case. There is no doubt that encircling a healthy cervix with a wire would be a comparatively easy affair, but amputation of the cervix is usually called into requisition for the removal of malignant disease, and when the part is about half destroyed by cancerous ulceration, or quite out of shape by a growth of adventitious tissue; it is by no means an easy matter to place a wire snugly around the part and keep it at the correct point, while it cuts through, and even when this part of the operation is properly attended to, there are other points which demand the operator's best attention.

The operation is performed thus: The loop being formed, and fixed in the cautery-electrode, is placed around the parts of the cervix to be removed; it is then drawn closely, and during the process of tightening, care must be taken to keep it on the point of severance, for if this be not attended to, it is very apt to slip, and when the part has been severed the operator finds that he has removed either more or less than he intended to.

Care must be also taken not to operate too closely to the vaginal attachment, or a peritoneal fistula may result. Formerly I used to place the patient on the back, and operate with a Byrne's speculum. For some time past, however, I have operated in Sims' position, and use Sims' speculum in preference to all others.

After the loop is in situ, and the vagina protected from burning by radiation or contact, the battery is attached, the loop brought to a proper degree of heat, and slowly tightened, until it cuts through, and the part to be removed is separated—the precautions alluded to under amputation of the tongue to be duly observed. The after-treatment is to be conducted on general principles.

Dr. John Byrne in his work on "Galvano-Cautery" says: "Those who confine their appreciation of this invaluable agent in uterine surgery to its blood-saving properties, omit to take into consideration its most attractive and important attributes. These consist, first of all, in the peculiar manner in which this hæmostatic effect is produced on the vessels, and which I surmise is in no way analogous to that effected by ligature, torsion, ecrasement, or styptics. Secondly, there are no disorganized blood clots or other effete material to become absorbed into the circulation. Blood-poisoning, as I have before observed, need not be apprehended as a sequel of cautery operations. In other words, it would appear that not only are the bloodvessels securely sealed up, but the lymphatics as well, and hence the immunity from hæmatoxic and inflammatory complications."

Dr. Byrne has probably had more experience with the galvano-cautery in uterine surgery than any other surgeon, and his opinion should carry considerable weight with it. In this connection I would state that I have observed in medical literature that those who have had the greatest amount of experience with the agent under consideration commend it highly, while those who know little of its merits, either pass it by in silence or discountenance its use.

CYSTIC DEGENERATION OF THE CERVIX UTERI.

When this disease is extensive, of course, the removal of the diseased part is the only treatment open to us; when, however, the cysts are few, and not so close together as to almost merge into each other, they may be separately destroyed by the cautery.

The cervix being fully exposed and freed from all moisture, the pointed cauterizer is brought to a little below a white heat, and each cyst is punctured separately, the cauterizer being held in the cyst until every portion of it is destroyed, which only occupies a moment or two. I have operated on several of these cases and all with success. It is a very simple operation, requires no preparation, and but little after treatment.

PEDUNCULATED TUMORS.

Mucous polypi and fibroid tumors that can readily be encircled by the loop may be removed after the manner described for amputating the cervix. In all cautery operations within the uterus, it is well to remember that the part operated upon is out of sight, and not as easily protected from burning by radiation as the parts heretofore under consideration. It is therefore essential to pause several times during an operation, lest the parts should become overheated, and, after the diseased growth has been severed, to at once disconnect the battery, lest on the removal of the instrument, the hot wire should come in contact with the cervix or vagina. In a former work* I have reported several cases in which large fibroids were removed by this method. Polypi of the nose, rectum or larynx may be removed in a similar manner, observing the same precautions.

AMPUTATION OF THE PENIS.

Dr. Bryant speaks highly of the cautery loop for amputation of the penis. The same rules apply to the perform-

---

* Electro-Therapeutics and Electro-Surgery, 2d edition, p. 261.

ance of the operation as do to the removal of the tongue
and cervix uteri. The after treatment, however, seems to
be of more importance. Contraction of the new meatus is
very liable to take place, unless kept well dilated mechani-
cally. Dr. Bryant says, that immediately after the operation, a catheter should be passed and left in; and, as the
wound heals, bougies should be introduced occasionally to
prevent subsequent contraction. I would suggest electrolysis after the manner described for the treatment of strictures. It ought to be successful, and if performed immediately after the amputation would, it appears to me, save
the patient and operator from further trouble. I regret
being unable to endorse the suggestion by experience.

HÆMORRHOIDS.

The treatment of hæmorrhoids by the galvano-cautery is
eminently satisfactory. It is never followed by pyæmia,
septicæmia or even hemorrhage: advantages that cannot
be claimed for any other mode of treatment. In my work
before alluded to, I recommended the operation to be performed in the following manner: "The rectum having
been cleared by an enema, the patient is placed on a table, in a position most convenient to the operator, and anæsthetized. The sphincter is then forcibly dilated, so as to
paralyze it. * * * This process will render the mus-
cle so powerless that it will not interfere with the process
of cicatrization. The next step is to seize the piles with a
pair of forceps and make gentle traction on them, bringing
them, if possible, below the sphincter. This is easily done
if the hæmorrhoids are large, pedunculated, and close to
the verge of the anus and together. Should such be the
case they may be encircled in one loop close to their attach-

ment, the loop heated, tightened, and all severed together."

Since the above was written, I have modified the operation as follows: The rectum having been emptied, I cause the patient to strain over a vessel of warm water, until the hæmorrhoids protrude. I then take each hæmorrhoid separately, and perforate with the pointed cauterizer at a dull, red heat. After all the piles have been so treated, they are smeared with oil or vaseline, and returned within the sphincter. The operation being a short one, a little nitrous oxide will answer for the anæsthetic. I have operated without an anæsthetic, on account of a patient refusing to take it, but, although the operation is quickly performed, it is painful while it lasts, and the involuntary contraction of the sphincter interferes. The advantages I claim for this operation over the one first described are:

1. It is much less severe and easier to perform.
2. It is not necessary to paralyze the sphincter.
3. There is less inflammatory action.
4. Very much less after-pain and less ulcerated surface to heal.
5. Full anæsthesia unnecessary.
6. After-treatment much shorter.

FISTULÆ AND SINUSES.

Fistula in ano may be treated by the galvano-cautery by two methods. First, by inserting a platinum wire into the fistula and bringing it out through the anus, the ends of the wire after being made fast in the cautery handle, the loop is heated and made to burn its way through the sphincter; the wound dressed and made to heal from the bottom as after the ordinary cutting operation.

The second method is to insert a slender dome cautery

into the fistula. It should be inserted cold and heated when in situ. It is made to burn until the pyogenic lining of the fistula has been quite destroyed. Before the operation is commenced, the sphincter should be forcibly put on the stretch, and held so for some minutes, so that its involuntary contractions may not interfere with the process of healing. An anæsthetic is always needed; I generally use nitrous oxide.

This operation answers the purpose fully as well as that first mentioned. There is practically no destruction of tissue, the after-suffering of the patient is almost nil, and the recovery much more speedy.

Fistulæ in other parts of the body may be treated on the same principle. I operated successfully on one case of recto-vaginal fistula, and on one of salivary fistula. The operation, however, is not so applicable to vesico-vaginal fistulæ, unless they be very small, for obvious reasons.

PROLAPSE OF THE RECTUM.

A V-shaped piece taken out of the protruding mucous membrane has been recommended for the cure of this trouble. I have no doubt it is quite effectual, but never have had occasion to perform it. It would be most readily performed with the cautery knife heated to a little beyond a dull red; the membrane being held in a clamp.

HERNIA.

An operation for the radical cure of hernia has been suggested by Dr. John C. Minor, of this city.* I give a description of the method to be pursued in the author's own words:

---

* Amer. Journal of Electrology and Neurology, July, 1879.

"The method I suggest is to form the adhesion by the galvano-cautery without invaginating any scrotal tissue, depending upon the natural or pathological tendency of all cicatrices produced by burns to contract and grow stronger and thicker by age. As compared with other adhesions they are firmer, less liable to absorption, and present to a remarkable degree the very conditions that are so essential for the radical cure of hernia. I would not trust to these alone in the beginning, but would urge the necessity of · closing the tendinous opening by wire sutures, so as to keep the protrusion, if possible, within the abdominal cavity. But if, in addition to this closure of the tendinous opening, we seal up the canal by firm cicatrices, it seems to me that the result must be far more certain than after the usual operation. The operation in brief, is as follows:

The hernia having been reduced, the internal ring is closed by silver sutures after Dowell's method. An incision is then made in the most depending portion of the inguinal canal, the cord and vessels clearly made out and covered with an ivory guard, that is passed in front of them and up the inguinal canal until it impinges upon the contracted ring above. The dome cautery, while cold, is next passed up the canal in front of the ivory guard, which separates it from the cord and vessels, until it meets with the obstruction at the contracted tendinous opening. First withdrawing the cautery a few lines, the spring is pressed, the cautery becomes red hot and is slowly withdrawn, thoroughly cauterizing the tissues in front of the cord, which is protected from impinging by the interposition of the ivory guard. In those cases where the weight of the hernia has drawn the external and internal rings until the orifices are nearly in apposition, the entrance and exit of the cautery should be at a point in the scrotum midway between the external ring and the most depending portion of the scrotum.

The silver wires should be left *in situ* for at least ten days, or until some necessity arises for their removal. In all other respects the treatment is to be conducted on general principles. The advantage of this method consists entirely in the difference between the contracting scar of a burn and the ordinary results of adhesive inflammation produced in other ways. The cicatrix once formed grows firmer with age, cannot be absorbed, neither stretches nor tears, but holds the tissues in a grip that never relaxes. So far as the immediate inflammatory action is concerned, following the operation, it might be more intense than that produced in other ways, but it is less likely to spread beyond the parts operated on, and offers the minimum amount of danger from septicæmia. There appears to me to be but one objection to the method, and that applies to the effect of contracting cicatricial bands upon the nutrition of the cord and its vessels. It is probable that if it acted at all to impair the nutrition of the parts, the slowness of action would lead to a gradual atrophy of the testicle. But I doubt whether any such result would occur. In the absence of practical experience it is impossible to determine whether this objection is of actual weight or of merely theoretical importance, and so, without further discussion, I leave the subject *sub judice.*"

NÆVI.

Nævi may be either burned out in toto by means of a suitably shaped cautery instrument, or may be tatooed with a sharp-pointed cauterizer at a bright red heat. The first operation is a simple one, the only care to be taken, is, to thoroughly destroy the nævus without encroaching on the surrounding or subjacent tissues. In tatooing a surface nævus, the operator has to employ great care and skill in making the punctures sufficiently close together, so that the inflammatory action which follows will take place over every point of the surface operated upon; otherwise the operation will not answer the purpose.

Although these operations will *cure* nævi, the scars resulting are far more marked than those after electrolysis properly performed, and before described.

THE SETACEUM CANDENS.

Tumors of various kinds may be treated by being transfixed with several platinum needles heated with a battery. The heat may be prolonged so as to cause the whole growth to slough, or the operation may be used simply to cause the formation of small eschars within the growth, which, acting as barriers to the blood supply, cut off a large portion of the nutrition. The operation is only applicable to cases where some destruction of the skin is no consequence.

To avoid the destructive action of the cautery on the skin, Dr. Jurasz, of Heidelberg, has suggested an operation which he calls subcutaneous galvano-cautery. The following is an extract from his article from the Medico-Chirurgical Quarterly for April, 1881:

"The subcutaneous galvano-cautery aims at the destruction of subcutaneous morbid growths *without burning or seriously injuring the skin*. It is, therefore, not only different from the so-called iguipuncture, but also from Middledorpf's *setaceum candens*.

"The subcutaneous galvano-cautery can be used in two different ways, either as *linear* or on an extensive plane. Both methods are very simple.

"In order to produce linear destruction of a subcutaneous growth by means of the subcutaneous galvano-cautery, a platinum wire is pushed through it and through the overlying skin. The ends of the wire are introduced into hollow needles of copper, the points of which are pushed slightly into the tissue to be destroyed. This accomplished, the copper needles are attached to a cautery battery by. means of conducting cords. As soon as the circuit is closed, that part of the platinum wire enclosed in the growth becomes incandescent and destroys the parts in its immediate neighborhood, *while the skin is protected against any lesion by the copper needles.* After the intended destruction has been accomplished, the needles are detached from the battery and removed; afterwards the wire is withdrawn.

"In the main, the process of cauterisation of an extensive plane is the same as the preceding, excepting that the wire is introduced in a circular direction, forming a loop around the growth underneath the skin. This is done very easily by means of a curved needle, when both ends of the wire are made to protrude from the same place. Then the ends are introduced into the hollow copper needles, the points of which are pushed into the growth as described in the other method. The ends of the wire have to protrude far enough from the hollow needles to screw them into an ecraseur. As soon as the electric current heats the subcutaneous platinum loop, it is tightened slowly by means of the ecraseur till the mass encircled by the wire is destroyed. After the current is interrupted, first the needles are unscrewed and then the wire is removed."

I have performed this operation three times, once on a nævus on the cheek, once on a cystic tumor in the auriculo-maxillary fossa, and once on a cystic growth on the fore-

head. In all three cases it answered the purpose as far as
the destruction of the tumors was concerned, and protected
the skin to a very great extent, but in each instance there
was a slight scar left, owing to the tubes holding the platinum wires becoming heated and slightly cauterizing the
skin.

THE CAUTERY AS A HÆMOSTATIC.

The use of the hot iron as a means of controlling hæmorrhage is too well known to need comment. The galvano-
cautery may be used as an efficient substitute, with this advantage, that the degree of heat can be controlled with
greater precision. It is most applicable to a general oozing
of blood from surfaces or parts inaccessible to the application of the ligature. A cautery instrument of suitable
shape should be heated to a dull red heat and applied. The
battery should be disconnected before removing the instrument from the bleeding surface, otherwise it sticks to the
flesh, which may be torn in the efforts to remove it, and in
consequence the hæmorrhage increased. By detaching the
battery, the instrument soon becomes cold, and may be
readily removed without tearing away the coagulum.

VARICOSE VEINS.

Obliteration of a varicose vein may be accomplished in
the following manner: The limb in which the vein is situated is to be tightly bandaged above the point selected for
operation. When the vein stands out full and turgid, it is
to be punctured with a thick, pointed cauterizer at a dull,
red heat. As soon as the amount of cauterizing has been
sufficient to form a firm coagulum, the battery should be
disconnected, and the instrument held *in situ* until cold,

when it may be removed, and the same procedure repeated at other points of the vein. Two or more veins may be operated upon at the same sitting. But little after-treatment is necessary, which may be conducted on general principles. Rest in the recumbent posture, however, should be insisted on for a few days following the operation.

Electrolysis has also been used successfully in the treatment of varicose veins. The modus agendi is similar to that already spoken of in the treatment of aneurism. The cautery is much to be preferred, however, as it is much more easily applied, makes a firmer clot and the effects are manifested more rapidly, and I would add that in the hands of those poorly skilled in electro-surgery, it is much more certain.

DETACHMENT OF THE RETINA.

Being impressed with the originality of the following article, taken from the *Medical News*, for January 28th, 1882, and being convinced of the usefulness of the operation described, I copy the article in full:

"Detachment of the retina, according to Dr. Abadie, is most frequently dependent upon a local cause, as it occurs ordinarily in cases of myopia associated with no diathesis whatever. It can therefore be treated by purely surgical means.

Clinical observation, pathological anatomy, and experiments on animals, show that the retina forms adhesions to the choroid whenever there are areas of spontaneous or provoked choroido-retinitis. If, therefore, such adhesion can be produced artificially, it can be hoped that the retina will be fixed to the underlying membranes. In order to produce the result, Dr. Abadie punctures the sclerotic and choroid with a delicate platinum knife, heated by the galvanic current, as far behind the ciliary region as possible. The ocular membrane, being thus perforated, the sub retinal fluid escapes, and an adhesive inflammation is produced, which maintains the retina in place. This method of treatment has been employed in eight different cases; in six instances of extensive old separation only slight benefit was produced, but in two cases where the detachment was limited, most satisfactory results followed. In no case was the reaction too violent, or have any unpleasant consequences occurred.

Struck by the considerable reduction of inter-ocular tension which remains after galvano-puncture of the eye, Dr. Abadie has made use of this method of treatment with the happiest results, in cases of glaucoma which resist treatment by iridectomy and sclerotomy." — *L'Union Medicale*, December 6th, 1881.

While one cannot but admire the ingenuity of the operation, it seems tolerably certain that electro-puncture with a needle from the negative pole, would answer the purpose equally as well as the cautery, and is more easily performed, and without the risk of destroying the surrounding tissues.

INSTRUMENTS.

The first essential in the performance of electro-surgical operations is a source of electro-motive force—a means of generating a current of suitable quantity and tension for the purpose in hand.

For applications to the surface of the body, where the skin forms a part of the circuit, the resistance is very great, hence we require a high electro-motive force, and but a small quantity of current. When, however, the integument has been punctured with needles representing the poles of a battery, the resistance is comparatively small, and therefore a high electro-motive force is not needed, but as in the majority of instances electro-puncture is employed for the sake of the chemical effects, it is essential that we should have a battery capable of transmitting a sufficient quantity of current to produce these effects in a given time. As long as we have an instrument that will do this, it matters but little how the current is generated. In surface applications, the dose of electricity varies on the average from $\frac{3}{1000}$ to $\frac{20}{1000}$ of a veber, whereas in cases where we wish to utilize the chemical effects of the current, the amount necessary may in some instances be as high as a veber.

It is therefore evident that, while surface applications need the utilization of a large number of cells, operations performed by electro-puncture need a very much smaller number of cells, but these should be of sufficient size to generate the necessary quantity of current. As this subject is not generally properly understood, and as we hear physicians constantly discuss the application of a current from a certain number of cells, without even knowing the electro-motive force of these cells, or the resistance of that portion of the body included in the circuit,—as if the number of cells alone, conveyed the idea of the amount of current transmitted ;—I have compiled the following table, taking Daniells' cell as a standard of electro-motive force, each cell representing one volt, and each having an internal resistance of four ohms, presuming the resistance of the portion of the body included in the circuit to vary from 1000 to 4000 ohms, which is a fair general average in surface applications.

Number of Daniells' Cells.	Internal Resistance of Battery.	Resistance of the Tissues in Ohms.	Current transmitted in Vebers.
10	40	1000	$\frac{1}{104}$
10	40	2000	$\frac{1}{204}$
10	40	3000	$\frac{1}{304}$
10	40	3000	$\frac{1}{404}$
20	80	1000	$\frac{1}{54}$
20	80	2000	$\frac{1}{104}$
20	80	3000	$\frac{1}{154}$
20	80	4000	$\frac{1}{204}$
40	160	1000	$\frac{1}{29}$
40	160	2000	$\frac{1}{54}$
40	160	3000	$\frac{1}{79}$
40	160	4000	$\frac{1}{104}$

It will be readily seen from this table that a battery of 40 Daniells' cells transmits only the same amount of current through a resistance of 4000 ohms, that 10 cells will transmit when the resistance is 1000 ohms; and as such differences of resistance exist, and vary according to the distance the electrodes are placed apart, the size of the electrodes, the conductivity of the particular kind of tissue through which the current is transmitted, the amount of moisture in the skin, etc., etc., it is evident that knowing the number of cells, is not knowing the amount of current transmitted.

Now let us consider the operation of electro-puncture, where the resistance of the circuit varies from 5 to 500 ohms, according to the distance the needles are placed apart, the conductivity of the tissues in which the needles are imbedded, the number and size of the needles, etc., etc., we will see how utterly inadequate such a battery is for the purpose.

Number of Daniells' Cells.	Internal Resist- ance of Battery.	Resistance of Tissues.	Current trans- mitted in Vebers.
10	40	50	$\frac{1}{9}$
10	40	40	$\frac{1}{8}$
10	40	10	$\frac{1}{5}$
10	40	5	$\frac{10}{45}$
20	80	50	$\frac{2}{13}$
20	80	40	$\frac{1}{6}$
20	80	10	$\frac{2}{9}$
20	80	5	$\frac{4}{17}$
40	160	50	$\frac{4}{21}$
40	160	40	$\frac{1}{5}$
40	160	10	$\frac{4}{17}$
40	160	5	$\frac{8}{33}$

It is very evident from this table that no increase of the number of cells will give a veber of current. It is also evident, that in order to get that amount of current, we must diminish the internal resistance of the battery, or rather employ a battery whose inter-resistance is not over one ohm. Stöhrer's battery fulfills this requirement. The electro-motive force of each cell is in round numbers about two volts, or equivalent to two Daniells' cells, and the internal resistance of each cell *of a suitable size* less than one ohm. These figures, although not exactly correct to a fraction, are practically sufficiently so. The subjoined table explains itself.

Number of Stöhrers Cells.	Internal Resistance of Battery in Ohms.	Resistance of Tissues in Ohms.	Current transmitted in Vebers.
2	2	5	$\frac{4}{7}$
5	5	5	1
10	10	10	1
10	10	50	$\frac{1}{3}$
10	10	100	$\frac{2}{11}$
20	20	300	$\frac{1}{8}$
20	20	20	1

Where we require a veber of current to do a work, and the resistance of the tissues is only five ohms, five of the cells just mentioned will be sufficient; but when the resistance is twenty ohms, we need twenty cells, and so on. The matter is purely a mathematical calculation based on the fundamental law of Ohm :—the current transmitted equals the electro-motive force divided by the sum of the resistances.

The great objection to this form of battery is that it is inconstant. It polarizes rapidly, and the exciting fluid becoming weaker through saturation, increases the internal resistance, and diminishes the chemical activity, and so the current generated becomes weaker. These defects may be practically remedied by having large negative plates and cells capable of containing a large amount of fluid (the cells usually found in the market are too small), and by using a rheostat to regulate the amount of current transmitted, so that as the battery becomes weaker (which fact is indicated by the galvanometer), the resistance can be diminished, and the current kept up to the desired point.

The simpler a battery is made, the better. The connections should be substantial and easy of access, so that each plate can be removed when requisite. When a rheostat is used, it is quite unnecessary to have terminal connections from *each* cell. I have had my instrument made with a binding post on the first and last cells, and use my rheostat for regulating the current.

For cautery purposes, where a battery is only used to heat a wire, or piece of platinum, or iridium, the resistance of the circuit being very low, and the intensity of the heat produced proportional to the square of the current transmitted, we need a battery of very much smaller internal resistance than those described. There are several useful forms of cautery batteries manufactured.

The Byrne cautery cell consists of a negative plate of thin platinum attached by its whole surface on one side to a plate of copper, the copper being backed by a plate of lead which is varnished so that only the platinum face is exposed. A single cell composed of two of these plates with a zinc for the positive between them immersed in bichromate fluid, and exposing twenty-two square inches of

FIG. 2.

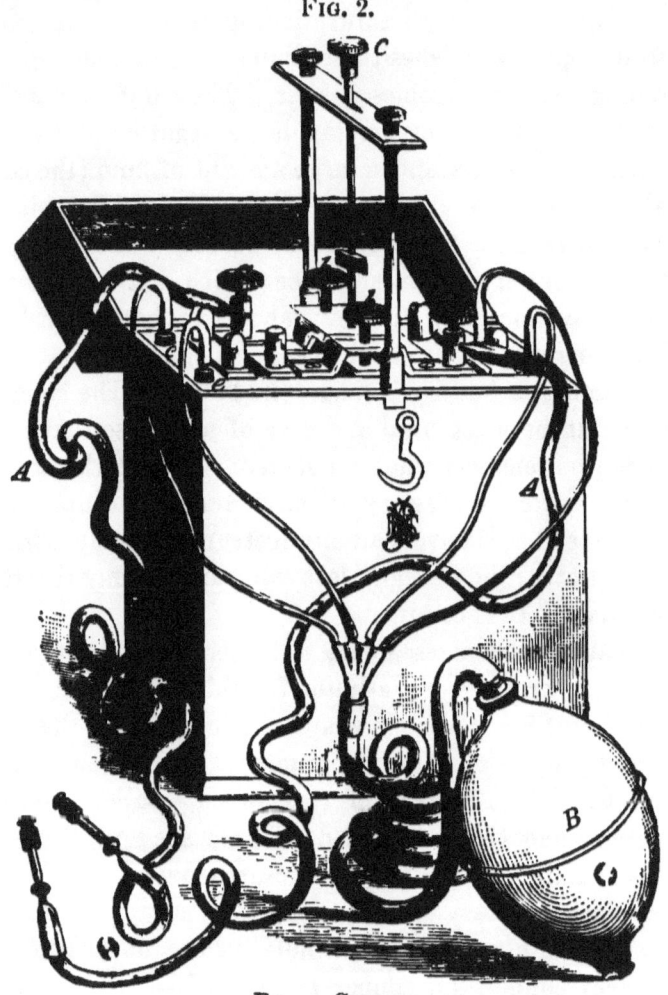

Byrne Cautery.

surface to the fluid, gives an electro-motive force of almost two volts and an internal resistance of less than one fourth of an ohm. Four of these cells constitute the cautery battery. Polarization is diminished by blowing air into the fluid by means of a rubber bulb and a divided hose, one nozzle for each cell.

This is an admirable battery for the purpose for which it is intended when properly constructed, but, as ordinarily furnished, the cells are too small and do not hold sufficient fluid, the platinum plates are too thin and (sometimes at least) so full of very small holes through which the fluid finds its way to the copper, that the battery soon becomes ruined—defects that could be remedied by a little care on the part of the manufacturers.

Dr. Piffard, of this city, has invented a cautery battery which is well and favorably known. It consists of six platinum zinc elements, immersed in the ordinary bichromate fluid, and arranged so that it can be used either in single or multiple arc. Polarization is checked by agitation of the elements themselves, which are so suspended as to be readily rocked to and fro by pressure of the foot of the operator. When carefully constructed this is a most useful instrument. The cells are large, each capable of containing about a pint of fluid.

The following wood-cuts represent a galvanic battery devised by Dr. B. F. Dawson, of New York City. It is composed of but two cells in each of which are two positive (zincs) and one negative (platinum) plate all measuring but four-and-a-half by six inches. The zincs (A) are perforated, and adjusted but half an inch apart, and between them a platinum plate is placed and held in position by uprights (B). On each side of the platinum plates are hard rubber

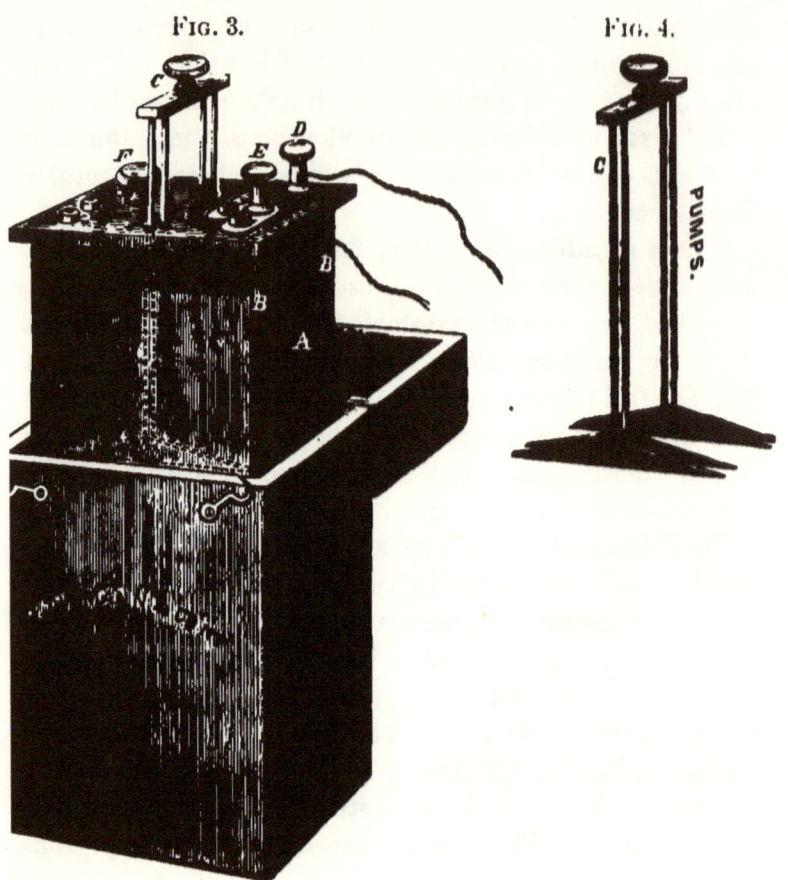

or celluloid pumps or agitators (*C*), to diminish polarization they are worked by means of a small knob. *D* and *E*
are two connecting screws, and *F* a knob for lifting the
battery out of the cells. The entire battery requires but
two and-a-half pints of fluid, with which amount it will
keep up a most powerful action, long enough for the most
prolonged operation, by the moving up and down of the
pumps (*C*), which, according to the intensity of the heat

desired, are moved more or less quickly. By this action, the old and exhausted fluid between the plates is thrown out through the perforations, and fresh fluid is made to take its place. This battery will heat a much thicker wire than either of those previously described, but will not heat so long a loop. It is very simple in construction and quite a serviceable instrument.

CAUTERY ELECTRODES.

These consist merely of suitable handles to hold the platinum to be heated, and can better be understood from the accompanying cuts than from any written description.

FIG. 5.

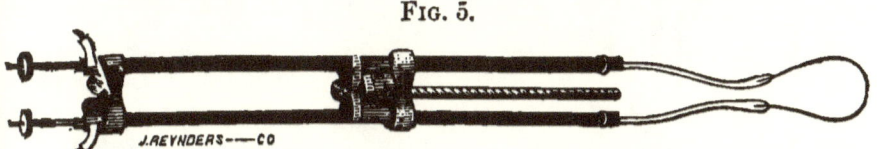

Byrne's Cautery Ecraseur or Loop Holder.

FIG. 6.

Byrne's Cautery for Cervix Uteri.

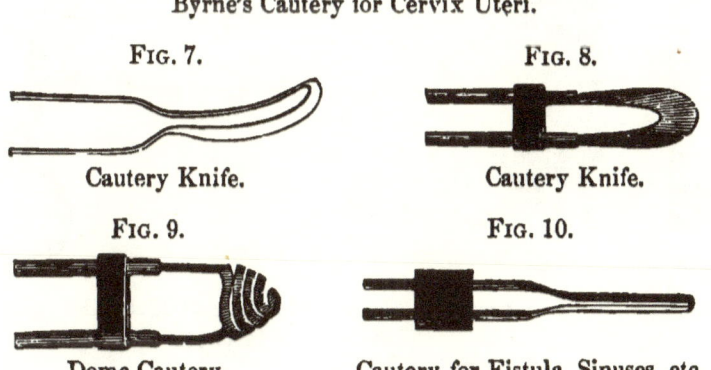

FIG. 7.	FIG. 8.
Cautery Knife.	Cautery Knife.
FIG. 9.	FIG. 10.
Dome Cautery.	Cautery for Fistula, Sinuses, etc.

FIG. 11.   FIG. 12.

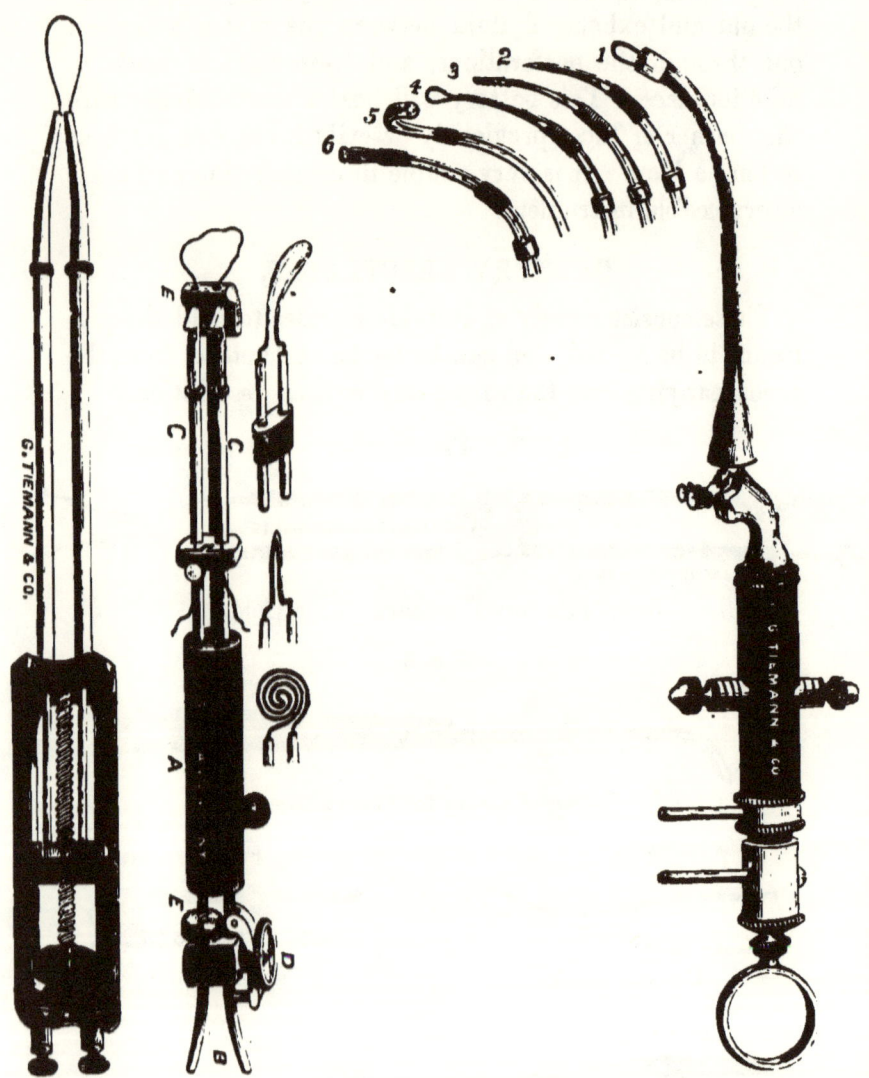

Dawson's Cautery Electrodes.   Cautery Handle and Electrodes, adapted for
                                              laryngeal operations.

THE RHEOSTAT.

This is a very useful instrument, and to those who wish to attain accuracy in the use of electricity, a requisite. Wheatstone's instrument is no doubt the best, and so well-known as to need no description here. It is very expensive, however, and in order to provide a cheap substitute, I have devised one which has stood the test of time and answers almost all purposes.

It consists of a plate of non-conducting material, on which is placed, either on the surface or in a groove, a film of plumbago or other suitable resisting material. One end of this resistant is connected with the battery, and the circuit is completed through a moveable key, one end of which is on the resistant, so that by changing the distance of the key from the extremity of the resistant joined to the wire from the battery, the amount of resistance is determined at pleasure.

In the accompanying drawings, Fig. 13 is a plan of the rheostat, Fig. 14 is a section of the same on line x x, and Fig. 15 shows a modified form.

Similar letters of reference indicate corresponding parts.

Referring to the drawings, A represents the bed-plate, supported on legs, B. It is made of hard rubber, slate, marble, glass, or any other suitable non-conducting material. In the upper surface of this table is a segmental groove, a, having at one end a slotted screw or stud, b, passed through the plate and joined underneath to a metal strip, c, the other end whereof is connected with the under end of the binding-post, d, to which the wire, d', is joined above. In this groove is placed a film of plumbago (indicated by a') or other suitable resisting material.

The key, C, for regulating the resistance, is composed of

FIG. 13.

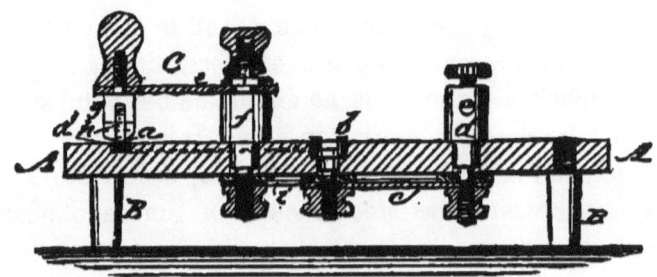

FIG. 14.

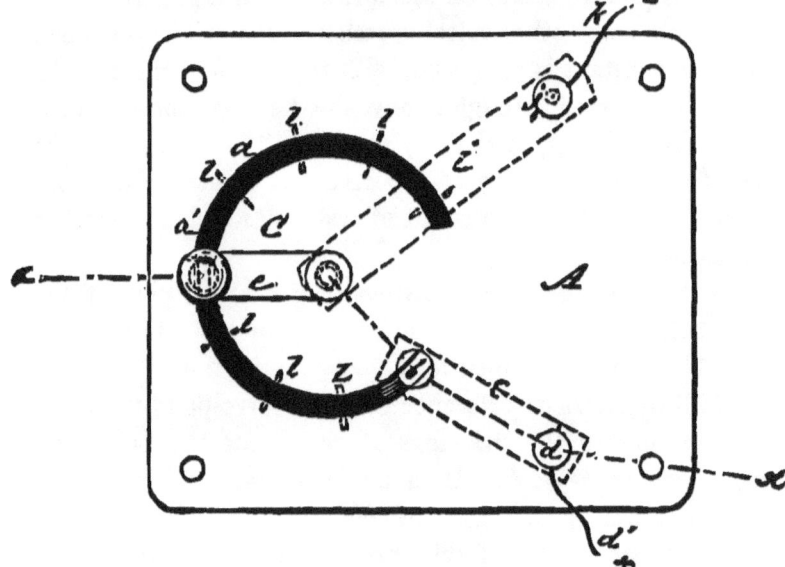

FIG. 15.

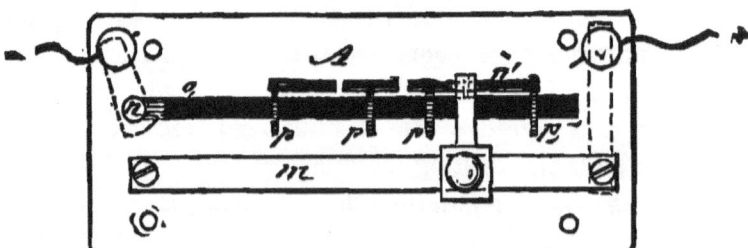

the horizontal arm, *e*, one end pivoted to the stud, *f* (the centre whereof coincides with the centre from the groove, *a*, is struck). The opposite end of the arm is joined to the right-angular stud, *g*, in the free end of which is pivoted a friction wheel, *h*, resting in groove, *a*, on the resistant, *a'*.
. The lower end of stud, *f*, projects through plate, *A*, and is connected with one end of metal strip, *i*, under the plate, the opposite end of said strip being joined to the binding-post, *j*, to which wire, *k*, is connected.

Across the groove, *a*, in radial lines, are placed strips of tin-foil, *l*, at regular or irregular intervals. These strips graduate the groove, and are intended to indicate the point to which the key must be moved in order to obtain a certain required resistance.

The operation of the instrument is as follows: When the key is turned so that the friction-wheel is in the slot in screw, *b*, the current flows from metal connection, *c*, through key, *C*, thence through metal strip, *i*, to wire, *k*. When resistance is required the key is moved over the groove until it reaches the point marked by the tin-foil strip indicating the number of ohms of resistance desired. Now the current has to flow through the resistant in the groove, *a*, before reaching the key, and thus the resistance desired is obtained.

In Fig. 15 a modification of the invention is shown. Here the groove is straight, lined with a film of plumbago or other resistant.

The arm of the key is slotted and passed upon the straight metal bar, *m*, so as to slide freely back and forth, and is provided with a set-screw to fix it in any required position on the bar.

The roller or wheel, *n'*, on the key, runs on the side of

FIG. 16.

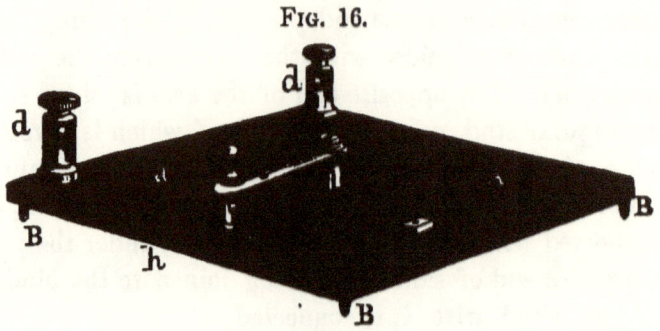

the resistant, o, but parallel to it. Narrow strips, p, of metallic foil, with right-angular end pieces, are placed across the resistant at right angles, so as to be crossed by the friction-wheel when moved back and forth. In this way the resistant is brought into the circuit. The foil strips serve to graduate the resistance, as before described.

The advantage of this arrangement is, that the plumbago, being free from the friction of the wheel, is not worn away, and thus its conductivity is not lessened, and greater accuracy is obtained. This arrangement may be applied to the segmental groove first described, as well as to the modification shown in Fig. 15.

FIG. 17.

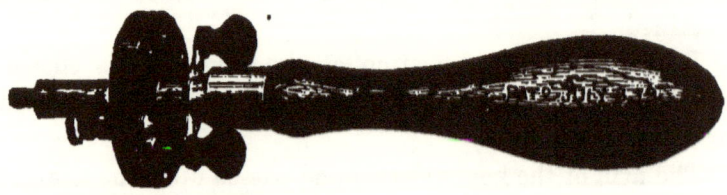

As a resisting medium I employ the film of plumbago, or else, where a very high resistance is required, a mixture of plumbago and sulphur, or plaster of Paris, made into a paste with a suitable cement.

Fig. 16 shows the finished instrument.

Fig. 17 represents the rheostat mounted on an ordinary universal electrode handle. This combination forming a very convenient instrument for general use.

THE GALVANOMETER.

A means of measuring the amount of current working, is a necessity in all cases of electro-puncture. A galvanometer, the deflections of which are accurately proportional to the current passing, and requiring the least amount of calculation to find the current in vebers, is of course the most convenient instrument to use. The tangent galvanometer has given me every satisfaction. In this instrument the tangents of the angles of deflection, multiplied by what is known as a constant — a figure adapted to each individual instrument — gives the current in vebers. The constant multiplier is furnished by the manufacturer with each instrument sold. For medical and surgical uses, a galvanometer should have at least two coils; one wound to about fifty ohms, for measuring currents passing through high resistances; one of five ohms for determining currents of larger quantity, to which might be added a band coil of one or two turns of copper ribbon, for measuring the current for cautery purposes. An effort has been made to manufacture a galvanometer that would indicate the current directly; that is to say, the figure on the dial to which the needle points would represent the current flowing. I have not as yet seen an instrument of this kind sufficiently accurate. It would be a matter of great convenience if one could be so arranged. It would obviate the necessity of referring to a tangent table continually. It is to be hoped that the future will develop such an instrument.

CONDUCTING CORDS.

A word must be said on the means of conveying the current from the battery to the work to be done. For purely medical applications, when we use small currents of high tension, the resistance of the conducting cord is a matter of no moment, hence the tinsel cords that are on the market answer very well; but for electro-puncture we need conductors having as little resistance as possible, hence it is necessary to employ a cord made of several strands of fine copper wire, insulated with silk, or rubber tubing, having the tags on the ends *well soldered on*, not tied as they usually are. These tags should be of such a size as to offer a good surface for connection. For cautery purposes these conducting cords cannot be too large.

NEEDLES, SURFACE ELECTRODES, ETC.

The operator should be provided with needles of various shapes and sizes to suit the different operations he may be called upon to perform.

Those depicted in Figs. 18 and 19 are those in general use. The needles intended to be attached to the positive pole should be made of unoxidizable material, either platinum or iridium. Gold or gilded needles do not answer. In operating on deep seated growths, where it is necessary to protect the skin from the action of the current, the part of the needles which are not intended for action should be insulated with a coating of hard rubber. This insulation may extend to within an inch or half an inch of the points, or more or less, as required for any special operation. When destruction of the skin is intended, the needles, of course, should be entirely uninsulated. For malignant tumors I use a flat spear-pointed needle made of

FIG. 18.   FIG. 19.

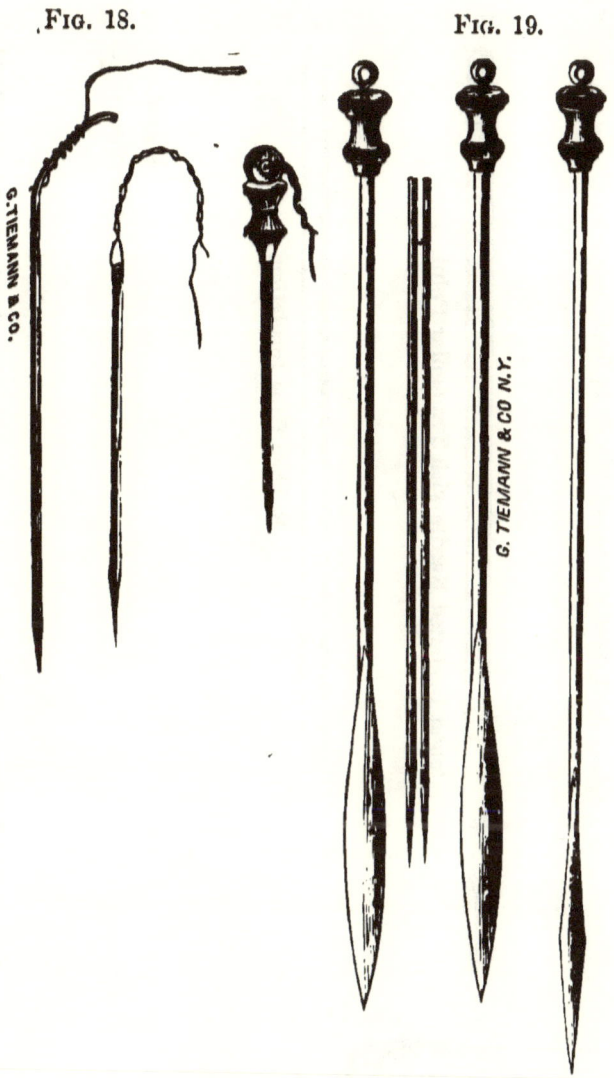

G. TIEMANN & CO.

G. TIEMANN & CO N.Y.

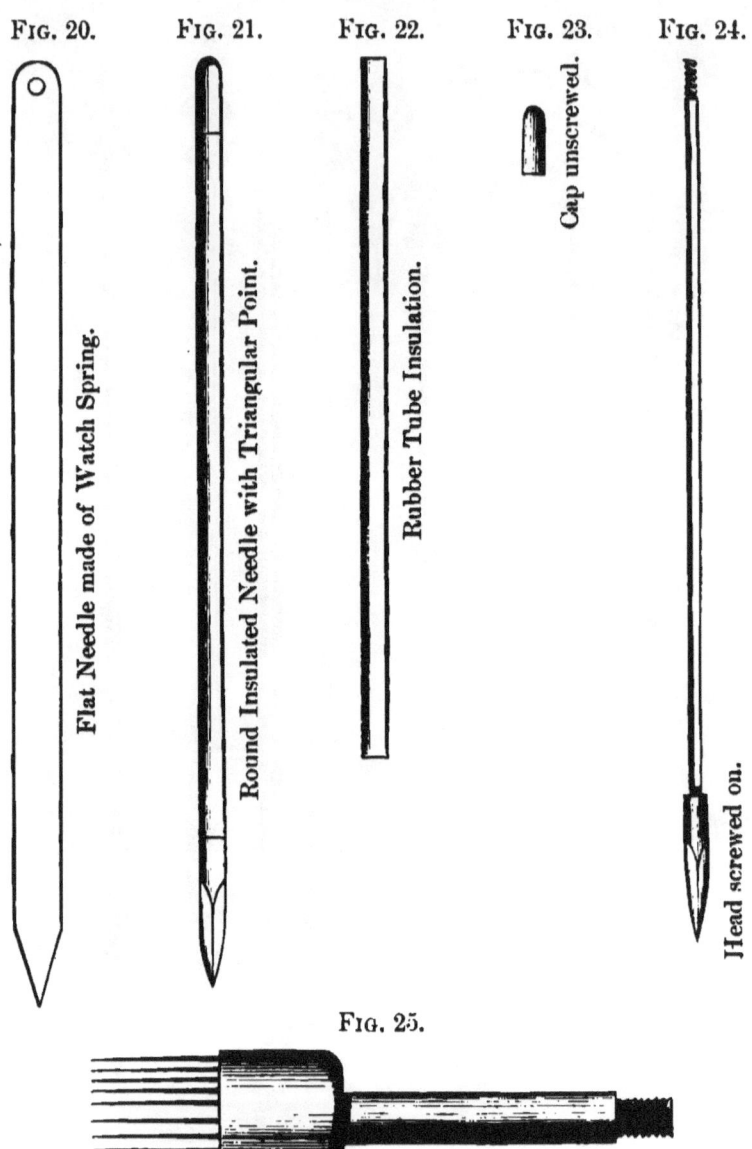

FIG. 20.   FIG. 21.   FIG. 22.   FIG. 23.   FIG. 24.

Flat Needle made of Watch Spring.

Round Insulated Needle with Triangular Point.

Rubber Tube Insulation.

Cap unscrewed.

Head screwed on.

FIG. 25.

Needles in Holder for Treatment of Superficial Nævi.

watch spring. I have chosen this shape because such a
needle is easily introduced and brings a large surface of
metal in contact with the tissue to be destroyed. See Fig. 20.

For large fibroid tumors, goitres, cysts, etc., I have devised a needle which is in every way satisfactory. It consists of a fine bar of steel, over which is slipped a slender
tube of hard rubber; on one end of the steel bar is screwed
an uninsulated triangular point of steel, platinum or iridium
which may be of such a length as to be adaptable to any special purpose, and on the other end a metal cap for attachment to the conducting cord: Fig. 21 shows the needle
ready for use, and Figs. 22, 23 and 24 the separate parts.
It is almost unnecessary to add that the base of the point
where it is screwed on to the shaft should be of the same
diameter as the insulating tube.

For small tumors, the ordinary electrolytic needles found
in the stores answer every purpose.

Fig. 26.

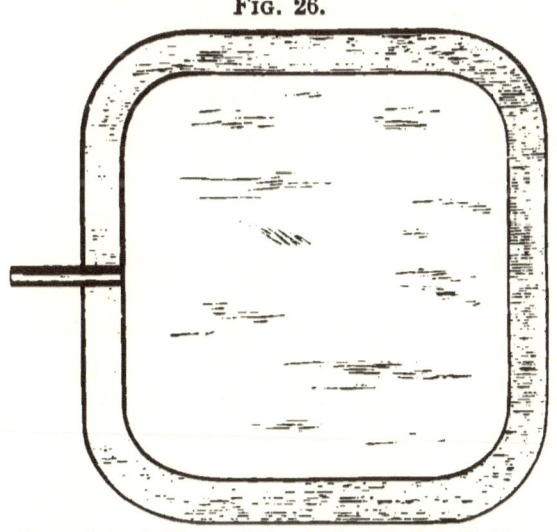

Chamois Pad Electrode backed with Soft Rubber.

When one pole of the battery is applied to the skin, I have found an electrode made of a flexible metal plate covered with chamois leather the most convenient. Fig. 26. It makes good firm contact, is easily bent into any shape and the covering is of much less resistance than sponge, and furthermore it is easily kept clean which is a matter of some importance.

THE ELECTRO-MASSAGE INSTRUMENT.

As this is a comparatively new instrument, it needs some description here, although only of limited utility in surgery.

FIG. 27.

It consists of a metallic roller, covered with chamois leather or other suitable material; an electro-magnet; and a permanent magnet, set in a strong frame which holds the instrument together. The roller, besides acting as the driving-wheel of the machine, is so arranged that it also acts as one of the electrodes, wherewith the current is transmitted, and is so connected by gear with the electro-magnet as to cause the latter to revolve its poles opposite those of the permanent magnet, which latter forms the handle of the instrument. Each revolution of the roller producing twenty-five revolutions of the electro-magnet, which is magnetized and demagnetized at each revolution, and so a current of electricity is induced, which is ample in strength for all purposes for which it is intended. The break-piece regulates the interruptions.

The circuit is completed by connecting any required electrode to the binding post, the roller acting as the other electrode: both are brought into contact with the surface of the body of the patient; and as the roller is moved about over the surface, the current is established and transmitted through the part over which the roller is made to revolve.

The instruments described constitute a very fair outfit for those who intend to practice electro-surgery.

All sources of electro-motive force which depend upon chemical action, are from their very nature open to many objections. For this reason the dynamo-machine is fast superseding the battery, in electric lighting, plating, telegraphy, etc., and will, no doubt, at a time not far distant, supplant the battery in medicine and surgery. I am now adapting the dynamo-principle to cautery, and hope shortly to be able to bring a satisfactory instrument to the notice of the profession.

INDEX.